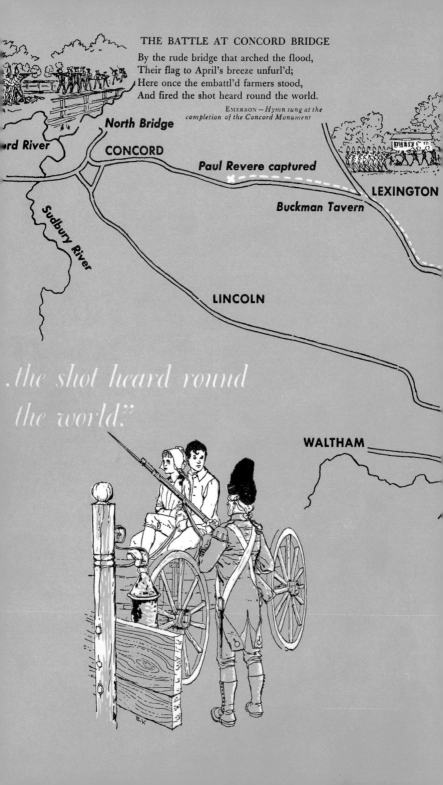

THE BATTLE AT CONCORD BRIDGE

By the rude bridge that arched the flood,
Their flag to April's breeze unfurl'd;
Here once the embattl'd farmers stood,
And fired the shot heard round the world.

EMERSON — *Hymn sung at the
completion of the Concord Monument*

North Bridge

rd River

CONCORD

Paul Revere captured

Sudbury River

Buckman Tavern

LEXINGTON

LINCOLN

*. the shot heard round
the world."*

WALTHAM

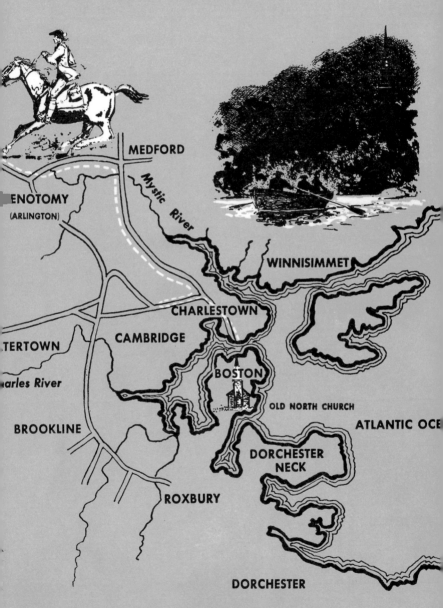

PAUL REVERE'S RIDE

"...One, if by land, and two, if by sea;
And I on the opposite shore will be,
Ready to ride and spread the alarm
Through every Middlesex village and farm,
For the country folk to be up and to arm."

LONGFELLOW

MEDFORD

Mystic River

ENOTOMY
(ARLINGTON)

WINNISIMMET

CHARLESTOWN

CAMBRIDGE

TERTOWN

arles River

BOSTON

OLD NORTH CHURCH

BROOKLINE

ATLANTIC OCE

DORCHESTER
NECK

ROXBURY

DORCHESTER

WE WERE THERE
AT THE BATTLE OF LEXINGTON
AND CONCORD

WE WERE THERE

AT THE BATTLE OF
LEXINGTON
AND CONCORD

By FELIX SUTTON

Historical Consultant: EARL SCHENCK MIERS

Illustrated by H. B. VESTAL

GROSSET & DUNLAP *Publishers* NEW YORK

© FELIX SUTTON 1958

FOR

Geoffrey

PRINTED IN THE UNITED STATES OF AMERICA
LIBRARY OF CONGRESS CATALOG CARD NO. 58-12567

We Were There at the Battle of Lexington and Concord

Contents

Illustrations

WE WERE THERE
AT THE BATTLE OF LEXINGTON
AND CONCORD

CHAPTER ONE

Captive City

SPRING had come early to New England in this year of 1775. Here it was, Rob Gordon thought, only the 17th of April, and already the grass was turning emerald green and the fruit trees and dogwoods were bursting into blossom. In any other year, the trees would still be stark and bare, with the fields showing smudges of dirty brown between patches of melting snow.

But this morning, driving down from Lexington in the one-horse wagon behind old Roman Nose, Rob had noticed that nearly all the farmers along the way had started their spring plowing. The pussy willows in the marshes and along the creeks were big, yellow-green furry balls. The robins and blue birds, early arrivals too this year, were chirping away merrily in the hedge-rows. There was a hint of April showers in the air, but when the brisk wind whipped away the clouds, the sun shone down warm and bright.

Rob slapped the lines sharply over his horse's back. The big bay broke into a lively trot, dragging the clumsy, springless wagon over the bumpy road in a series of jolting bounces.

"Mercy sakes, Rob!"

Sary Williams, sitting on the hard, wooden seat beside him, clutched at the side of the wagon to keep from being pitched out into the ruts of the road.

Rob laughed. "I reckon old Roman Nose must be feeling that extra measure of oats I gave him this morning."

He gathered up the lines in his big, strong, long-fingered hands and settled the bay down to a steady jog.

Sary's answering laugh was as light and gay as the trilling songs of the birds. She was a slight girl, the top of her head hardly coming to Rob's broad shoulders. Her long hair was the color of ripe wheat in the fall. This, along with her fair skin and blue-green eyes, was in sharp contrast

[4]

to Rob's dark-skinned features and his unruly shock of coal-black hair.

In the big, leatherbound family Bible that lay on her mother's desk, Sary's name had been inscribed thirteen years ago as Sarah. But ever since she had been old enough to recognize her name when she heard it spoken, family and friends alike had dropped the letters "a h" from the end of it and substituted "y." And so she was Sary. Sary Williams, daughter of the widowed housekeeper at Mr. John Buckman's tavern on Lexington Green, and happy and excited now at the prospect of spending a day and a night in the big city of Boston.

Rob and Sary had grown up together. Ten years ago, when Rob was only a little tyke of five, both his parents had died of a strange sickness that swept across the Massachusetts Bay Colony. Rob had been adopted by big John Buckman, his father's best friend. For three months, every winter since, he had studied in the little one-room school run by Professor Mather for the children of Lexington Town and the surrounding farm families. The rest of the time he worked around the tavern as stableboy, serving boy,

[5]

gardener, and jack-of-all-trades. Next fall, John Buckman had said, Rob would enter Harvard College over in Cambridge.

The wagon jolted into the streets of tiny Roxbury Town. A group of children, playing tag on the village green, waved and shouted, and a small black-and-white dog rushed out into the street and tried to nip at old Roman Nose's heels. The big bay, without breaking his stride, lashed out with a cow-kick that sent the dog sprawling. Yelping indignantly, it ran into the nearest yard and disappeared behind the house. A man who was spading a kitchen garden laughed as the dog ran past him, and waved a friendly hello to Sary and Rob.

Then they were past the town and heading out onto the Neck, a narrow strip of land not much wider than the road itself, that connected the town of Boston with the mainland. A hundred yards ahead, they could see the barricade which the British soldiers had thrown up across the road. Half a dozen Redcoats were marching in orderly strides back and forth in front of it, their bayoneted muskets held stiffly erect against their shoulders. Two or three others lounged around idly, apparently off duty.

[6]

"Do you think we'll have any trouble getting through?" Sary unconsciously lowered her voice as she asked the question.

Rob grinned. "Not when I tell them we're taking supplies to their army in Boston."

"But what if they find out that the supplies we're carrying aren't for the soldiers at all?"

"Don't worry your pretty head about that," Rob said, still smiling. "The Lobsterbacks are the stupidest soldiers in the world. Mr. John Hancock said so himself in the tavern just last night. Look how many times our dispatch riders, like Paul Revere and Billy Dawes, have slipped by them. I'll wager if I told them we had driven this wagon in from the moon, they'd wave us through the gates, and we'd be safe in the Green Dragon before they remembered where the moon was."

"Just the same," Sary whispered, "you be careful." She inched over in the seat a little closer to Rob and tucked her hand under his arm.

Rob noticed the gesture, but he didn't say anything. It's a man's job, he thought, to protect women in dangerous times like these. Suddenly he felt strong enough and sharp enough to outfight or outwit any Redcoat soldier in the world.

[7]

He knew, of course, that these indeed were very dangerous times. The siege of Boston, the high-handed treatment of the American colonists by the English King George, and the fact that the whole countryside might explode into armed revolution at any hour were the chief topics of discussion in the public room of Mr. John Buckman's tavern every evening. As he served the steaming cups of hot buttered rum and Dutch tea to the men gathered around the tavern's fireplace, Rob listened to every word that was spoken. The two men he liked to listen to most were Mr. John Hancock and Mr. Sam Adams. Both were leaders in the patriotic organization known as the Sons of Liberty, and it was said that the British General Gage had offered a reward for their capture dead or alive.

Mr. Hancock, who was tall and young and dark-haired and always richly dressed, laughed about the reward money. But Mr. Adams, who was older, and whose hands shook with some sort of palsy, and who was always shabbily clothed, looked mighty serious when it was mentioned. Rob didn't blame him. He reckoned he'd be real bad scared if the English put a price on *his* head.

The whole trouble, Rob knew, had started a

great many years ago when the Americans had objected to paying taxes to the King without being represented in the English Parliament. And it had come to a head, the fall before last, when a group of colonists, dressed up like Red Indians, had dumped a shipload of English tea into Boston Harbor in protest against the tea tax. After the "Boston Tea Party," as Mr. Hancock liked to call it, General Thomas Gage, who was the military governor of Massachusetts as well as commander in chief of the British army, had closed the city up tight.

He had stopped all shipping. For more than a year not a Yankee trading vessel had entered or left Boston Harbor. Even the ferries to Charlestown and Cambridge had been put out of business. This single road across the Neck was Boston's only means of communication with the outside world. And now it, too, was blocked by the King's soldiers.

No question about it, Boston was a captive city. Dozens of fast schooners and sloops, once the backbone of New England's proud merchant fleet, lay tied up at the idle wharfs, their canvas rotting and their bottoms collecting barnacles. Business in the town had slowly ground to an almost complete standstill. Hundreds of able sea-men and skilled workers wandered idly through the city's crooked streets and loafed their days away on the waterfront. There was little food in the town, and most families went hungry oftener than not. But these men stubbornly refused the only work that was to be had, the building of bar-racks for Gage's Redcoat army.

As a result of this shortage of permanent quar-ters, the British army of occupation was scat-tered all over Boston—living in warehouses, abandoned tanneries, empty storerooms, and the spare bedrooms of nearly every private home.

Under the terms of the Quartering Act, a law bitterly detested by all of Boston's people, a red-coated Quartermaster Sergeant might pound on any citizen's door at any hour of the day or night:

"In the King's name, you are forthwith or-dered to furnish lodging, light, heat, and food to three private soldiers of the Royal Welsh Fusil-iers!"

Or it might be two lieutenants of the Oxford-shire Light Infantry . . . or the 17th Dragoons . . . or the 24th South Wales Borderers . . . or soldiers from any one of the dozens of Redcoat regiments that kept Boston under their thumb.

And when this summons came, the citizen had to crowd his family into smaller quarters and make room in his house and at his table for the unwelcome guests.

Boston, in fact, all of New England, was like a teakettle coming to a boil over a hot fire. Nobody knew when the lid would blow off, but when it did, it was certain to go with a bang.

All of these thoughts were crowding Rob's head as he pulled old Roman Nose to a stop before the town gate. A British Grenadier, resplendent in full-dress uniform, marched up to the wagon, swaggering self-importantly.

"Well, now," he said, looking Rob and Sary over carefully. "And where might the two of you be bound for?"

"If you please, sir," Rob answered meekly, "we have a load of cured hams, salt pork, and potatoes for the regiment quartered in Clark's warehouse down on Ship Street." He knew well enough that you didn't address a private soldier as "sir," but Mr. Hancock had said that it never hurt to butter up the Lobsterbacks; it made 'em easier to fool.

"Oh, have ye now?" The soldier raised an eyebrow under his bushy hat. "Let's see. That

[11]

A British Grenadier marched up to the wagon

would be the 5th Northumberlands, wouldn't it?"

Rob looked innocent. "Why, no, sir. Unless I've mistaken my instructions, it's the Dorsetshires that are barracked there."

The Grenadier guffawed loudly and slapped Rob on the arm. "Ye're a smart lad," he said. "Too smart to try to fool a British soldier. I was just testin' ye. If you'd agreed that the Northumberlands were at Clark's, I'd have known that somethin' was fishy. That's me own regiment, and we're camped up near the Common. So I allow ye're honest enough. But just the same, I'd better have a look."

Sary sat silently as the man stepped to the back of the wagon and rummaged through its contents. Rob winked at her, grinning, but he maintained a respectful silence.

You had to hand it to the Redcoats for one thing, he thought, as his eyes examined every detail of the soldier's uniform. Even the privates were always smartly turned out.

The Grenadier wore a tall, black bearskin hat with a polished brass plate in front. His scarlet coat was heavy and bulky, with bright green lapels that extended all the way from his shoulders

[*13*]

to his knees. It looked mighty hot and uncomfortable for such a warm spring afternoon. His breeches and knee-length leggings—or spatter-dashes, as the British called them—were covered with a moist, white paste known as pipe clay. Rob had heard that unless the breeches were always immaculately pipe-clayed and shining, an English soldier was severely flogged. But just the same, he thought, it must be real uncomfortable to go around all the time wearing trousers that were sticky and never quite dry. The soldier's hair was thickly powdered and tied up with a black ribbon in a queue that hung down over the back of his neck. There was a faint dusting of the white powder on the shoulders of his coat.

By now, the man had satisfied himself that Rob's wagon contained nothing more dangerous to the British army than food. He reached into a pocket in the long tail of his coat and extracted a soiled piece of paper which he handed to the boy.

"Ye'll be needin' this pass to leave the town unless ye come back while I'm still on duty."

"We're planning to spend the night in Boston and go back home in the morning," Rob said.

"Well," the Grenadier said, motioning for the

[*14*]

sentry at the barrier to open the gate for them, "see that ye keep out of mischief."

"Oh, we'll be careful to do that, sir."

Rob took a cloth bag from under the seat and offered it to the soldier.

"Here are some apples that have been ripening in our root cellar all winter. Mayhap you and your men will enjoy them."

The soldier took the bag, his eyes shining. British army rations, as everyone knew, were very bad and rarely plentiful. The apples would be a welcome treat; and it never hurt to do a small favor for a British sentry. You might want a big one in return some day.

"Thankee! Thankee kindly, lad!" the Redcoat smiled. "Now get along with ye!"

Rob touched Roman Nose with the lines, and the wagon rolled through the gate and across the Neck to the cobblestones of Orange Street that led into Boston Town. They bumped out of Orange Street, down Marlbrough Street, past the old State House, and into Union Street. Rob pulled up in front of a large brick tavern. Above the door hung a big figure of a fire-snorting dragon that had been hammered out of a sheet of copper. It was green with verdigris and age.

[15]

The Green Dragon was one of the favorite meeting places for the Sons of Liberty. Rob had heard Mr. Hancock say that more revolutionary plots had been hatched in its back rooms than in any other place in the whole of the American colonies. He wondered why General Gage hadn't closed it up long ago. But apparently the British High Command could have the wool pulled over its eyes as easily as the common soldiers. Now, as the wagon came to a stop under the dragon sign, the short street was deserted.

Rob jumped down onto the cobbles and turned to offer Sary a helping hand. As he did so, a large, fat man, a white apron covering his ample stomach, came out of the tavern. His broad, rosy face was creased into a jolly smile. A woman, almost as round and ample as himself, followed close behind.

"Well, I declare!" the woman said, beaming. "How you two tykes have grown! Rob, lad, you've sprung up this winter like a young sugar sapling! And, Sary, I do vow that you're getting prettier every day you live!"

She folded the girl in her big arms and gave her a mother-bear hug. "Now come right in this minute and have a cup of hot tea!"

[*16*]

Rob shook the tavern keeper's hand warmly. "I've got the food supplies here that Uncle John promised to send you, Mr. Sullivan," Rob said, as he watched Sary and Mrs. Sullivan dis-

appear into the inn. "But we'd best get this wagon unloaded before a Lobsterback patrol comes along and confiscates it."

The host of the Green Dragon lifted the canvas covering from the wagon's bed.

"Glory be!" he said warmly. "All these victuals are a sight for sore eyes! You folks who live out in the country are almighty fortunate, with no scarcity of food to fret about. But here in Boston, what with the bloody British blockade and all, we've been on short rations lately. These will come in mighty handy. Now just you drive round to the back door, and I'll send Jerry out to help you unload."

As Mr. Sullivan was speaking, Rob's ears caught the sound of the slow-paced tread of a squad of British soldiers coming down the street from the direction of Dock Square. There was no mistaking the clomp-clomp-clomping of the hard leather heels of the Regulars stamping against the paving stones.

He jumped into the wagon seat.

"Never mind Jerry," he said. "Send him back to the barn."

He clucked softly to Roman Nose, and the horse moved quietly down the street. At the next corner, Rob turned him sharply left, then left once more into an alley.

There he drew the wagon up and waited.

[*18*]

CHAPTER TWO

The Fight

ROB stood by Roman Nose's head, stroking the horse on the muzzle and speaking to him softly to keep him quiet.

He heard the Redcoat patrol go by, their footsteps clattering off into the distance. When all was quiet again, he drove the wagon down the alley to the barnyard behind the Green Dragon. Jerry was waiting for him.

In ten minutes, the wagon had been emptied of its precious cargo and the supply of food safely put away in the Green Dragon's storeroom. Jerry, the towheaded stableboy, led Roman Nose away to unhitch him, feed him, and bed him down for the night.

When Rob entered the public room of the tavern at Mr. Sullivan's heels, it was already beginning to grow dark. Tallow candles smoked and guttered in their holders above the long, wooden tables that lined the walls.

Mr. Sullivan led the way to a small table in a corner. "Sit ye down, lad," the big man said, "and have a bowl of hot fish chowder while you tell me all the news from up Lexington way."

There was no sign of Sary. Now and then Rob could hear a burst of tittering and giggling from somewhere up in the top part of the house. So he judged she was upstairs gossiping with the Sullivans' twin daughters, who were about her own age. You could certainly trust womenfolk to keep their tongues clacking at a rate that would beat Old Harry, especially when they hadn't seen each other for nearly a year!

Rob dug into the steaming bowl of chowder. His normally hearty fifteen-year-old appetite had been sharpened by the long ride through the crisp spring air. The fat tavern keeper sat down on the bench beside him.

"We hear you folks had a little excitement up to Lexington yesterday," he said.

"We had a bit of it, sir," Rob replied between mouthfuls. "Mr. Paul Revere came riding into town just as church services were letting out. He said General Gage might be sending out some soldiers to capture our stores of powder and food, and to arrest Mr. Hancock and Mr. Adams. You know that they've been staying in Lexington with Mr. Hancock's cousin ever since they escaped from Boston."

"Yes, I knew that. What happened then?"

"Well, sir, you can bet we were all busy the rest of the day. We hid the cannon, the powder, and the sacks of bullets out in the woods. Then we scattered the food stores. We put 'em in attics, barns, woodsheds, anywhere we could think of."

He grinned as he pictured the British army searching for supplies that had vanished into thin air.

"The Redcoats couldn't find 'em now if they looked from here to Christmas. Then about a dozen of us saddled up and rode all around the country, taking word to the militia companies to have their guns handy and be ready to march as soon as they hear the signal."

"And what's the signal to be?"

[*21*]

"Church bells, sir. Mr. Revere said he'd ride back and warn us if the Regulars decide to attack. Then we start ringing the bells in Lexington. When they hear us over in Concord and Acton, they start ringing *their* bells. Then the next town picks it up. And the next. I can tell you that if Gage sends the Redcoats to Lexington, they'll have a surprise waiting for them."

Rob finished the last of the chowder and sopped out the wooden bowl with a thick slice of bread.

Mr. Sullivan chuckled, his fat, aproned front shaking merrily.

"For a man who's forbidden to leave Boston," he said, "Paul Revere does a mighty lot of riding around the country."

Rob flashed white teeth in a big smile.

"It's a wonder the Redcoats haven't arrested him long since."

"It is for a fact," Mr. Sullivan agreed. "General Gage suspects that he's the chief messenger for the Liberty Boys. And he is, too. But the general can't catch him to prove it. Just the same, to be on the safe side, Gage gave orders during the winter that Paul's not to be issued a pass out of town under any circumstances."

The innkeeper slapped his broad stomach and chuckled again.

"But that doesn't stop Paul Revere. Not one little bit it doesn't. He keeps a skiff hidden out in the reeds down by the Charles River. So whenever he has a dispatch to carry, he just rows across to Charlestown, right under the nose of that British man-o'-war that's patroling out there. Then he borrows a horse on the other side, and away he goes!"

"Wasn't it Mr. Revere who rode up to Fort William and Mary last winter to warn the militia about—"

As Rob spoke, a shadow fell across the doorway that led to the street. Mr. Sullivan laid a restraining hand on his arm.

"Sh-h-h! Lobsterbacks!"

Three British soldiers entered the tavern. They wore the same high bearskin hats as the Grenadier who had stopped Rob and Sary at the town gate. Talking and laughing loudly, they strode into the room. They hung their hats on wooden pegs stuck into the wall and then slumped down on a bench that ran the length of a long table on the other side of the room from Rob and Mr. Sullivan. They unbuttoned the collars of

"Sh-h-h! Lobsterbacks!"

their bulky coats and stretched their legs under the table. One of them began to pound loudly on the tabletop with his clenched fist.

"Landlord! Landlord!"

Mr. Sullivan jumped up from the bench beside Rob, who was now almost hidden in the lengthening shadows of the corner. Rubbing his hands on the front of his apron, he hurried over to his new guests. He beamed the disarming smile with which he customarily greeted all British soldiery.

"Yes, gentlemen! Welcome to the Green Dragon! We are at your service!"

"We hear the word, Landlord," one of the Grenadiers said in a loud voice, "that you mull the spiciest hot buttered rum in Boston."

"I trust you will find that correct, gentlemen."

"Then bring out a sample!" the soldier roared. "Bring out *three* samples! We're celebrating!"

Rob shrank back into the shadows, trying to remain unnoticed, as the soldiers talked and laughed. Their voices boomed across the room.

"So the colonel and me," the biggest soldier was saying, apparently picking up a story he had been telling when the trio entered the Green

Dragon, "got all dressed up like Yankee farmers and started out for a stroll through the Rebels' country to see what we might see. The colonel was wearing a fine pair of polished boots and had a lace handkerchief in his sleeve. He sputtered when he talked like a macaroni straight out of Whitehall Palace, and he wouldn't have fooled anyone who wasn't both deaf and blind."

The Grenadier laughed loudly as he remembered the spectacle of a proper colonel of the British army trying to pass himself off as a crude Yankee clodhopper.

"So by the time we got to Watertown, the colonel was all tuckered out, and we stopped in a tavern for dinner. 'Miss,' he said to the serving wench who brought our food, 'do ye have any idea where a pair of honest workmen could find employment in this neighborhood?'

"Well, the lass gives him one look. Then she says, 'Colonel—for by the way you talk you're either a colonel or a gen'ral—you'll find employment to spare for yourself and all of Gage's men before the summer is gone!' "

The three soldiers exploded into a torrent of laughter.

"So then what did the colonel do?" the second man asked, wiping the tears from his eyes with the back of his hand.

"That just about wound him up," the first man said. "We got out of that inn fast, and then the colonel decided he'd had enough. He said he was heading back to Boston, but for me to go on ahead and learn anything I could. He said there'd be a commission in it for me if I succeeded."

"Well, now," the third soldier said, grinning and slapping the storyteller on his broad back. "Mayhap we'll live to be takin' off our caps to Leftenant John Howe yet, before this Yankee war is done."

"Maybe you will." Private John Howe grinned. "But I'm not countin' my epaulettes before they're safe on my shoulders."

"Then you went on after the colonel left?" one of the men prompted.

"Then I went on," Private Howe said. "Being an honest North Country lad with none of the airs of a London coxcomb, I passed for what I said I was. A deserter. I told the Rebels that gun smithing was my trade. At Worcester I saw enough powder and guns to blow up Gage's

[27]

whole army. Then I went to Concord and saw the same thing. A Rebel, Major Buttrick, put me to work repairin' muskets. But I'd seen all I needed to see, so one evening I faded quietly out of the town and came back here to report."

Rob, sitting in the shadows that were growing darker by the minute, strained his ears to catch every word. So the Redcoats had spies out! And they knew about the powder stores at Concord and Worcester!

Meanwhile, Mr. Sullivan had brought in three steaming cups of the spicy hot buttered rum and set them on the table.

"Away with ye, Landlord!" one of Private John Howe's companions growled. "We're talkin' private business."

Mr. Sullivan hurried back into the kitchen. If he took notice of Rob sitting hunched back in the corner seat, he gave no sign.

"I wrote a report to General Gage," Private Howe went on, "and then he sent for me."

"Go on with you," the second soldier said. "The gen'ral sent for you himself?"

"He did that. I was ushered into a big room

at Headquarters, and there was General Gage and his whole staff.

" 'John, me boy,' he said, just like I was as good as anyone in the place, 'you're going to be an officer soon, so it's just as well that you get used to officers' company.' "

The others whistled.

" 'John,' the general said, 'do ye think we could get to Worcester safely, destroy the stores, and then return to Boston?'

" 'General Gage,' says I, and I knew my commission depended on my answer so I determined to give him a straight one. 'General,' says I, 'Worcester is nigh fifty miles from here. The countryside is hilly. The roads are narrow and crooked. The Rebels are determined. If you were to march a column of ten thousand Regulars to Worcester, and if you had a train of artillery to go with 'em, I don't think a man-jack of your army would get back alive.' "

"Whew!" One of the soldiers picked up his pewter mug and drained it off. "Then you think the Yankees are that set on fightin'?"

"I do, Caleb. And don't you forget it if you

have to go up against 'em." Private John Howe paused for a moment and then went on with his story.

"So then the general says, 'What about Concord, John?'

" 'General, sir,' I said, 'Concord is a different kettle of fish. You could send out a fast column by night, arrive in Concord before daybreak, burn the stores, and be safe back in Boston before the Rebels knew what had hit them.'

" 'Then Concord it is, gentlemen,' the general said. 'And here's something for you, John, in payment for your sharp eyes and quick mind.' And with that he took a purse from his pocket and tossed it to me."

Private Howe leaned back in his seat and took a leather bag from his pocket. Even from across the room, Rob could hear the jingle of the coins as he shook it.

"So Concord it's going to be, my bucko boys. And now let's spend some of the general's gold for another of the landlord's mugs."

"When d'ye think it'll come, John?" Caleb asked.

"Any day now. Mayhap tomorrow, or the next."

Rob felt his heart pounding so hard that it made a throbbing ache in his throat. A raid on Concord! Maybe tomorrow! This was news that had to be carried out of Boston fast! He tried to melt himself farther into the black shadows, where he could stay lost from sight until the Redcoat soldiers were gone. When he moved, his elbow brushed against the wooden bowl on the table in front of him. It clattered to the floor.

The three Grenadiers jumped to their feet at the same instant Rob did. They knocked over the long bench as they pushed their table out from the wall. The tallest and biggest one, the man John Howe had called Caleb, leaped across the room and grabbed Rob roughly by the front of his coat.

"What 'ave we 'ere?" he roared. "A Rebel spy, I'll be bound! Eavesdroppin' on 'is betters!"

Rob tried to struggle free from the Redcoat's heavy grip. He was nearly as tall as the man, but Caleb was heavily built, and thick in the arms and shoulders. He shook Rob hard, so hard that

[*31*]

the boy's teeth rattled. Rob pushed against the soldier's chest with both arms. Still holding on to the coat with one huge, hamlike fist, Caleb slammed the knuckles of his other hand into the side of Rob's face in a back-lashing slap that made his head swim.

"Here, Caleb! Here now!" Through his half-daze, Rob recognized the voice of Private Howe. "Don't be so rough with the lad. Could be he means no harm."

"He overheard every word ye said, John. We'd best take 'im to the sergeant."

"That's true, John," the third Grenadier agreed. "Let the sergeant decide what's to be done with him."

Rob's mind raced in panic. He couldn't be arrested! Not now! Not now that he knew about the coming raid on Concord!

He swung his fist wildly in a booming arch and caught Caleb flush on the eye. With a surprised howl of pain, the big soldier flung the boy from him. Rob stumbled backwards, fighting to keep his balance. His body banged sharply against the side of a big stone fireplace, and his head, snapping back, crashed into the stones of the overhanging mantelpiece. A shower of sparks detonated before his eyes. Through the blur, he

saw Caleb's huge bulk rushing at him, his great fists swinging like the vanes of a windmill and his voice roaring in rage.

Rob put his hands against the stones of the fireplace behind him to steady himself. His fingers touched an iron poker, and then closed over the handle.

As Caleb rushed in, Rob swung the poker savagely at the man's head.

The wild blow landed, with a sickening crunch, just above the soldier's ear. He stopped as though he had run head-on into a stone wall. His arms dropped. His mouth flew open. A stupid, vacant look glazed over his eyes. Then he slowly slumped to the floor like a sack that has been emptied of grain.

For the split part of a second, Caleb's two companions stood frozen into inaction by this sudden, violent turn of events.

This was all the time Rob needed. He dashed for the open doorway and disappeared into the dark and deserted street.

CHAPTER THREE

Escape!

ONLY a few faint lights were showing along the length of Union Street when Rob's racing feet hit the cobblestones outside the door of the Green Dragon. For the most part, the whole neighborhood was bathed in inky blackness. Rob wheeled and ran for the shadow of a house two doors away. He ducked around the corner of the house, then stopped and peered cautiously back at the tavern.

A pale square of soft light spilled out of the open door and glinted off the green copper of the dragon sign. One of the Grenadiers appeared in the puddle of light and looked searchingly all around.

"It's as black as Old Nick's pit out here," Rob heard him say over his shoulder. "Ain't no telling where the rapscallion went."

He was answered by a voice from inside the inn.

"No use tryin' to find him, John. You'd best come back and help me with Caleb. He's real bad hurt."

The figure of John Howe turned and disappeared from sight.

Rob took off his shoes and tucked them under his arm. Then, walking quietly in his stocking feet and keeping well hidden in the shadows, he made his way to the end of the square.

He turned left on Ann Street and then left again into a narrow alley behind the row of houses. At its end, he came to the stable yard in the rear of the Green Dragon. He climbed a high fence and scouted carefully around the side of the stable to make sure no one was in sight. Then he walked swiftly to the box stall into which young Jerry had put Roman Nose.

He spoke softly to the horse to quiet him and, opening the half-door, slipped into the stall.

He was no sooner inside than the kitchen

door of the tavern opened and Mr. Sullivan appeared. Behind him came the two Redcoats supporting the wounded man between them. Rob laid a reassuring hand gently on the bay's soft muzzle.

"The horse trough is right over here, gentlemen," Mr. Sullivan said. "A dash or two of cold water should bring your friend around."

"If the blow from that poker didn't addle his brains for good!" one of the Grenadiers growled. "You stay close by, Mr. Landlord! We'll settle with *you* next!"

Rob watched, fascinated, as the soldiers bathed their comrade's bloody head. Caleb groaned and mumbled and then, suddenly, straightened up and shook his head like a big, shaggy dog that has just come in out of the rain.

"O-w!" He raised one hand to his temple and then jerked it sharply away as his fingers touched the bruised and aching bone. "Ow—ow-w! Me 'ead's killin' me!"

For the first time one of the Redcoats laughed.

"I venture it'll need more than a Rebel poker to dent that thick skull o' yours!"

Rob breathed a sigh of relief. He'd been

[*37*]

afraid he had killed the man. But Caleb appeared to be coming around rapidly. He caught sight of Mr. Sullivan and then, seeming to remember what had happened to him, his face turned red and his features twisted in a furious rage.

"Nab that man, John!" he roared. "We're in a hornet's nest o' Rebels!"

He started forward, but John Howe put a hand on his shoulder.

"Go easy, Caleb."

"Gentlemen," Mr. Sullivan said in a consoling tone of voice, "I tell you again I didn't know the lad was there. He came in earlier off the street, begging for a bite of food. I gave him a bowl of soup, gentlemen, and left him. Likely he dozed off to sleep and woke up after you came in."

"That was no call to brain me with a poker!"

"Ye'll have to confess, Caleb," Private Howe said, "that ye gave the lad a rough cuffing about."

"He was likely frightened into panic," the landlord suggested. "Our young people of Boston have had rough going of late."

"In any case," John Howe said, "we'll gain

[38]

nought by staying here. We'll give the boy's description to the Provost Marshal, and I wager he won't get far."

Rob waited, crouched in the stall, until the men had gone back into the kitchen. A few moments later he heard the three Grenadiers leave the tavern and walk up the gloomy, silent street outside, their boot heels clopping on the rough cobbled pavement.

He waited quietly for another hour, and when there was no sign of a British patrol come to investigate, he crept to the kitchen door.

"Mr. Sullivan!" Rob kept his voice low, though its tone was urgent. "Mr. Sullivan!"

The door opened, and the innkeeper peered out into the darkness.

"It's me! Rob Gordon!"

"Come in, boy! Come in quick!"

Rob hurried into the kitchen, panting from pent-up excitement. The landlord closed the door behind him.

Mr. Sullivan's face broke into a broad, pink-cheeked fat-man's smile.

"So our little gamecock has come back to roost!

[*39*]

You came near reducing the size of the King's army by one. But what caused the ruckus, laddie?"

Rob told him about the conversation he had overheard. The landlord's smile faded, and his face grew grave as he listened.

"So you see, I couldn't let them take me, Mr. Sullivan," Rob said. "If they're planning a surprise raid on Concord, we've got to let the people know so they'll be ready."

"Good work, Rob," the landlord said. "And quick thinking, too, as well as fast action. I'll see that word gets to Dr. Warren tonight. Then we'll think about getting you safely out of town and back home."

He opened the door and called in the direction of the stable:

"Jerry! You, Jerry! Come here!"

In a few minutes the towheaded stableboy appeared, rubbing sleep from his eyes. His back and shoulders were covered with wisps of hay, and Rob judged he had been sleeping in the loft. He gave no sign that he had heard the commotion at the watering trough.

"Wake up, lad," Mr. Sullivan said. "I want

you to carry a message. Do you know the house of Dr. Joseph Warren around on Hanover Street?"

The boy nodded.

"Then kindly step over there and tell the good doctor he's needed here. Tell him Mrs. Sullivan has been taken by the vapors."

When the lad had departed on his errand, Mr. Sullivan winked and said:

"Jerry's a good lad, though a bit on the dull side. What he doesn't know he can't talk about, should he be stopped by a Redcoat patrol."

Rob had heard of Dr. Joseph Warren. Next to John Hancock and Sam Adams, he was the most important man in Massachusetts on the side of the Rebel cause. And he was a marked man in the eyes of the British authorities. But in spite of the threat of a hangman's noose, he remained in Boston to provide a link with the leaders who had been forced to flee. The British allowed him to stay because he was Boston's finest doctor, and the English army needed medical care as well as the people of the town.

In half an hour or less, Dr. Warren appeared in the public room of the Green Dragon, his black satchel in his hand. Peering from behind the kitchen door, Rob was surprised to see that, like Mr. Hancock, the doctor was young and tall and handsome and had a dapper air about him. Mr. Sullivan led him immediately up the stairs as though to pay a professional visit to the ailing Mrs. Sullivan.

After a short while they came down again, walked across the public room, and entered the kitchen.

Dr. Warren extended a hand to Rob and gave him a friendly smile.

"So this is our young firebrand? I understand that, single-handed, you laid the British army low."

Rob grinned in spite of himself.

"Rob Gordon," he said, "at your service, sir."

"Well, Rob Gordon, you did a fine service for the cause of Liberty this night. One you may well be proud of. And you may tell your friends in Lexington and Concord that before the British come a-marching, Paul Revere will come a-riding ahead of them."

He nodded to Mr. Sullivan and went out.

"Now, lad," the landlord said to Rob, "we had

best start thinking about *you*. It would never do for you to get yourself nabbed betwixt here and the town gate."

"Did Sary—?" For the first time since the excitement had begun nigh two hours ago, Rob thought of the girl. "Did Sary—?"

Mr. Sullivan's grin interrupted the question.

"Your Sary and the girls are safe in their featherbeds upstairs. They heard the scuffling down here, but I told 'em it was just a pair of roisterers. Time enough for them to know about you after they've had a sound night's sleep."

He extracted a huge gold watch, as big as an oversized turnip, from his pocket and consulted its face.

"H-m-m! Nigh ten o' the clock! Sunrise will be about five. And by that time, you and Sary and the wagon should be approaching the gate. Get ye up in the hayloft, away from prying eyes, and catch a few winks. I'll see to it you're aroused in good time."

Rob said good night, went out to the stable, climbed the ladder into the loft and buried himself deep in the sweet-smelling hay. His mind flashed back over the abrupt events of the eve-

ning. He'd have to get back to Lexington as
soon as he could, and . . .

Before the thought could be completed, Jerry
was shaking his shoulder.

"Time to get up, Mister Rob. The master says
come straight to the kitchen."

[*44*]

Rob jumped to his feet, brushed hay from his hair, and scrambled down the ladder. The night was as black as when he had climbed up.

Sary and the Sullivan twins were eating breakfast at the kitchen table. Mrs. Sullivan was bustling about the big room with remarkable agility for a woman of her size. The landlord himself stood in the doorway.

"Grab yourself a bite, lad," he said. "We've got no time to dally."

Sary looked up as he seated himself beside her at the table.

"Rob!"

There was a frightened look in her eyes, like that of the young doe Rob had come upon unexpectedly one morning in the woods. He remembered that instead of throwing his musket to his shoulder and firing, he had loudly said: "Boo!," and the doe had vanished with a flick of her white tail into the thicket. He wondered what Sary would have to say if she knew that, at the moment, he was comparing her to a doe.

He patted her small hand.

"It'll be all right, Sary. Eat your breakfast and don't worry."

When Rob had polished off a steaming bowl

of cornmeal mush he got to his feet. Sary had already finished, and now she was standing by the door wrapped in a heavy cloak, evidently one of Mrs. Sullivan's, that enfolded her little frame like a tent. Mr. Sullivan entered from the public room carrying an old green-black felt hat of the kind favored by New England country men.

"Likely this will be too big for you," he said. "But it will help serve as a disguise, happen the Redcoats are looking for a black-haired, bareheaded boy."

Rob put the hat on his head. Its wide brim flopped down over his ears.

Mr. Sullivan grinned at the sight.

"More's the better," he said. "You don't look like much of anybody in that rig. And now it's time to be off."

Mrs. Sullivan hugged Sary. The twins hugged Sary. Mrs. Sullivan wiped a tear from her eye with her apron hem and gave Sary a dozen messages to carry to her mother. Then they were all out in the stable yard.

Old Roman Nose stood hitched to the wagon, sniffing the cool morning air and stamping his hoofs in the hard-packed dirt. Mr. Sullivan lifted Sary up bodily and deposited her on the wooden seat. Then he turned to Rob and patted his shoulder affectionately.

"Be careful, lad. Likely no one will spot you, but it's best to take no chances. Drive slow, and attract no attention to yourself."

Rob climbed into the wagon and picked up the lines.

"And give my regards to John Buckman."

Mr. Sullivan sniffed the wind, and winked.

"It smells a mite like rain this morning. So tell the boys in Lexington and Concord to keep their powder dry."

The first pale rays of the rising sun were streaking the sky over Boston Harbor as Rob, hunched over in his seat under the slouch hat, drove Roman Nose along Orange Street toward the town gate. Half a dozen wagons and farmers' carts were lined up ahead of him when he finally pulled up to the barrier. There was a great deal of argument about passes, and the sun, coming up suddenly as it does in mid-April, was well over the horizon by the time it was Rob and Sary's turn to go through.

The sentry at the barricade was the same one who had passed them into the city yesterday afternoon.

"Well, well," he said cordially. "Ye got rid of yer load o' victuals, I can see. If the boys down at Clark's warehouse enjoyed 'em as much as me and my lads relished the apples you so kindly gave us, ye're welcome back in Boston any day."

Rob handed over his pass. The man took it, but he seemed to be in a friendly, talkative frame of mind, unwilling to let a new-found friend leave without a few more words.

"That must be yer grandpappy's hat ye're wearin'," he laughed. "It's a genuwine Rebel lid. Here, let's have a look."

With a playful gesture, he reached up and lifted the hat from Rob's head. Rob sat bolt upright in surprise. In the same instant he heard a yell from one of the other sentries:

"Hold there! Hold there! It's the Rebel boy from the Green Dragon Inn! Stop him!"

Rob thought he recognized the voice of Private John Howe.

At the soldier's outcry, the guard at the barrier leaped to swing the heavy gate shut. Rob leaned forward and gathered up the long leather lines in his hands.

"Hang on, Sary!" he shouted.

He brought the ends of the lines down in a stinging slash across Roman Nose's rump.

"*Hiy-yo! Ho!*"

He swung the leather in a swift arc and slashed down again.

"*Hiy-yo! Roman Nose! Hup!*"

At the first shock of the whistling leather, Roman Nose gathered his powerful legs under him and sprang. By the time the lines stung him again, he was off and running like a racehorse. Sary hung onto the jouncing seat with both hands. Rob stood with bent knees, his lean body arched forward over the singletree like a chariot driver's, the lines gripped firmly in his left hand as his right arm swung their long ends down over the horse's rump and back.

"*Hiy-yo! Roman Nose! Ho!*"

They flashed through the gate an instant before the barrier slammed shut.

Then they were racing across the Neck toward the safety of Roxbury Town.

Behind them the dull boom of a musket shot echoed in the still air.

CHAPTER FOUR

Mr. John Hancock

THE wagon dashed into Roxbury with Roman Nose at a dead run. Halfway through the town, Rob slowed the horse to a fast trot. Roman Nose tossed his head and tugged at the reins in protest. He wanted to run. But Rob knew there was a good twelve miles or more between them and John Buckman's tavern in Lexington. Being a good horseman, he wanted to save the big bay's strength in case he needed it.

"But you're a whole lot of horse!" Rob thought admiringly as he held him back with a firm, steady pull.

Old Roman Nose was all of that. He was what the New England farmers called a "country

[51]

horse." He could pull a plow or a wagon all week. Then on Sunday, hitched to a buggy, he could sedately take the family to church and look stylish doing it. Under saddle, he could keep up with the best Virginia-bred hunters—although staid New Englanders frowned upon so frivolous a sport—and Rob was sure that, over the distance, he could run the heart out of the new-fangled English Thoroughbreds that some of General Gage's officers had brought with them to Boston.

The fact that he was called old Roman Nose had nothing to do with his age. When he had been foaled, six years ago, John Buckman had taken one look at him and said: "He has a nose like an old Roman." So Rob had named him Roman Nose, and the "old" just seemed to come naturally.

Sary hadn't said a word since they had raced so suddenly away from the British barricade. It had been all she could do to cling to the bouncing, pitching wagon. Now that they had slowed down to a decent pace, she pulled the clumsy bonnet off her head, shook out her long, grain-golden hair in the morning sunlight, and turned round in the seat.

"Now, Mr. Rob Gordon, will you be so kind as to explain?"

"Explain what?" Rob was glancing back over his shoulder to see if there were any signs of pursuit. There were none. And there probably wouldn't be, now that they were safe on the mainland. Long before the sentries at the town gate could send into Boston headquarters for a mounted officer—and then explain to him why he should ride out after a farmer boy's wagon without first getting an order from his commanding colonel—they would all be safe in Lexington. Thank goodness, Rob thought, the English were such a thorough people! Still, it did no harm to keep a watchful eye cocked backwards.

"Explain *what?*" Sary echoed. "Why, explain what all this foolishness is about!"

Rob jerked his attention back to the moment at hand.

"Mrs. Sullivan told me you had some trouble with the Redcoats. That's why we had to leave Boston so early. At first I was—sort of scared. But now I'm startin' to get *mad,* Rob Gordon! I'll bet that was you having a fight in the public room last night. And with the Redcoats, I shouldn't wonder! And now all this yelling and screaming and shooting back yonder at the gate!"

Rob grinned.

Sary didn't often display her temper. Normally, she kept it well hidden behind her green-blue eyes. But now those eyes were flashing sparks.

"Robert Buckman Gordon! I'm simply just going to bust wide open if you don't tell me what's been going on behind my back!"

Rob chuckled at her outburst. And then as the wagon rolled on through the pleasant country lanes, he told her everything that had happened since the three Grenadiers had come into the Green Dragon the evening before.

"So you see, Sary, I *had* to whack him with that poker. I couldn't do anything else. I had to let Mr. Sullivan and Dr. Warren know about the plans for the raid on Concord."

The sparks in Sary's eyes had softened as Rob talked. They were still there, but now she was smiling. A few drops of rain had started to fall from a sky suddenly turned cloudy. Rob pulled the collar of his jacket up around his neck.

"Here," Sary said. She spread out the huge folds of the cloak Mrs. Sullivan had given her. "We can both keep dry under this."

[54]

Rob pulled half the cloak over his shoulders, and the two rode close together on the wagon's seat as the April rain came showering down.

The village clock was striking nine as Rob pulled the wagon around Lexington Green and stopped in front of the Buckman Tavern. The early morning rain had stopped, and on the smooth, closely cropped grass of the square, the Lexington militia company was going through its drills. The drillmaster barked his commands in a clipped cockney accent, and the militia men, shouldering an odd assortment of old muskets and fowling pieces, were doing their heavy-footed best to execute them.

Rob handed Sary down from the seat and ground-hitched his horse. Then the two hurried into the tavern.

Big John Buckman stood behind the long bar, idly polishing a pewter mug. Mr. John Hancock sat at a nearby table, enjoying a late breakfast of biscuits and Dutch tea, and leisurely leafing through a sheaf of papers that were spread out before him.

"Ha!" John Buckman's voice boomed. "The travelers have returned! How do things fare in Boston?"

The Lexington militia company was going through its drills

At this last sentence, Mr. Hancock looked up from his reading.

"So, Rob, you have been to Boston? Do you bring any news?"

"I'm afraid, sir, that I've brought back some most important news."

"Indeed?" Mr. Hancock pushed the papers away from him. "Then pray sit down and join me in a cup of tea, and tell us all about it."

John Buckman stepped out from behind the bar.

"Sary," he said to the girl, "take off that ridiculous cloak. And then I think your mother may have need of you in the kitchen."

He sat down at the table beside Rob and Mr. Hancock.

"Now, young sir," John Hancock said, "let us have this important news."

Once again, Rob told the story from the beginning. The adventures of the Redcoat spy . . . the planned attack on the ammunition stores at Concord . . . his fight with Caleb . . . the incident at the town gate this morning. As Rob talked, John Hancock's face grew serious.

"We knew that open war was bound to come," he said gravely when Rob had finished telling his tale, "even though most of us had hoped, without much hope, that it could somehow be avoided. But it would seem that the British won't have peace except upon their own terms. And I fear that they are terms which free men will refuse to accept."

"Do you think we should start ringing the alarm bells, John?" Mr. Buckman asked.

"No, no. I think not yet. The British may march tonight, or tonight a week. There's nothing to be gained by alerting the countryside and possibly keeping every farmer in the county standing idly by while his fields are in need of plowing."

"But, sir," Rob put in. "That Redcoat, Private Howe, knows that I overheard him tell the British plans. He knows that I escaped from Boston. With that knowledge, may not General Gage decide to march at once?"

John Hancock grinned. "I doubt very much if friend Howe will go to his commanding general and confess that he has been wagging a loose tongue about military secrets in a public tavern. If the attack comes sooner than originally planned, rest assured that it will not be because of that talkative gentleman. No. I think we can rely on Dr. Warren and Paul Revere to alert us in good time."

"None the less," John Buckman said, "it is time for you and Mr. Adams to make yourselves scarce in Lexington."

"If there's to be war, I'm of a mind to stay right here and help fight it," John Hancock said.

"Nonsense, John!" The tavern keeper slammed his hand down on the table top with such force that the teacups rattled in their saucers and the tea slopped out on the polished wood. "Any able-bodied man's hand can pull the trigger of a musket. We need more than John Hancock's trigger finger. We need his brains and his vision and his leadership if our country is ever to be free!"

"My good friend," John Hancock said, laying a hand on his host's sleeve, "that was a most eloquent and complimentary speech. I thank you. Yes—you're right. Each one of us has his work to do. And I know as well as you what mine must be."

"Then we will have no more foolish talk, John." Mr. Buckman turned to Rob. "Lad, go ask Mrs. Williams kindly to pack Mr. Hancock's trunk."

Rob leaped to his feet.

"Before you do that errand, son," John Hancock said, "would you mind doing one for me? Run over to the Reverend Clark's house and ask Mr. Adams if he will be kind enough to meet me here at his convenience."

As Rob dashed out the tavern door and up the road to the big white house of Reverend Clark, where Mr. Adams was staying, the crisp commands of the militia drillmaster rang in his ears:

"Po-ort—*harms!*"

CHAPTER FIVE

Paul Revere Rides

IT WAS ten of the clock, and Rob was getting sleepy. The excitement of the night before, the mad dash out of Boston this morning, a full day's work catching up with the chores he had neglected yesterday—added to the fact that he had got only a few scant hours of sleep in the hayloft of the Green Dragon—all combined to make his eyes heavy and his head nod as he tried to busy himself serving refreshments to John Buckman's guests.

There was an unusual number of men in the tavern's public room for so late an hour. When Rob's news had been reported to the militia company, most of the men had decided to spend the night in Lexington rather than return to their farms. It had kept Rob and John Buckman jumping to serve dinner to them all. And Sary and her mother had been equally busy in the kitchen preparing it.

Now, as Rob sat on a stool behind the tavern's bar, his chin slumped forward on his chest, and his eyes closed.

He was awakened by John Buckman's hand gently shaking his shoulder.

"Rob, lad, forgive me. We've been so busy that I clean forgot the hour. It's been a big day you've had. Now off to bed with you and leave the tavern's business to me."

Rob mumbled his thanks and wearily climbed the stairs to his small room just overhead. He took off his shoes and stretched out on his cot.

"I'll rest for just a minute," he thought, "before I get undressed."

Instantly, he slipped away into a sound and dreamless sleep.

At the same time Rob was climbing the stairs to his room, in Lexington Paul Revere was walking up the broad stone steps of Dr. Joseph Warren's fine home on fashionable Hanover Street in Boston. He rapped quietly on the big door. It was opened almost instantly by Dr. Warren himself. Paul entered quickly, and Dr. Warren closed the door behind him.

"Well, Paul, it has come. A detachment under Lieutenant Colonel Smith and Major Pitcairn is marching on Lexington and Concord tonight."

Paul Revere smiled. He was a thick-set, stocky man, heavy of arm and shoulder, round of face and square of chin. He did not look like the finest horseman in Massachusetts—which he was.

"I am afraid, sir, that you are the second person who has brought me that news tonight," Paul Revere said.

"And the first?" Dr. Warren inquired.

"A stableboy from the Province House who had been ordered to ready the officers' horses for the march."

Now it was Dr. Warren's turn to smile. "I fear it is difficult for the British to keep many secrets, with nigh half as many soldiers in Boston as there are citizens. None the less, we must alarm the militia and Minute Men in Lexington and Concord, and in all Middlesex County as well."

"How are the British marching," Paul asked, "by land or by sea? I have promised Colonel Conant of the Charlestown militia that I would signal him ahead of time by means of lanterns hung in the tower of Christ's Church."

"And your signal?"

"One light if the column marches by land across the Neck. Two, if they take boats to Cambridge and march from there."

"Then two lights it is, Paul. The boats are already loading."

The two men shook hands warmly.

"Be careful, Paul," the doctor warned. "I'm sending Billy Dawes to ride by way of Boston Neck. One of you *must* make it through. I pray you both do."

"And what of you, sir? When this pot comes to boil, it may well mean your neck."

"I'll have to risk that. Now, God speed you, Paul."

Paul Revere made his way quietly from Dr. Warren's house to Christ's Church, the building with the highest spire in Boston. Robert Newman, the sexton, was waiting for him.

"Two lights, Bob," Paul whispered.

Without a word, the sexton went into the

darkened church and began to climb the steep stairs that led to the belfry. He carried an unlit lantern in each hand.

Paul hurried down the hill to the riverbank. His skiff, with Joshua Bentley and Thomas Richardson already seated at the oars, was waiting. As the boat pulled away from the marshy shore, its oarlocks muffled with the torn remnants of Mrs. Bentley's best petticoat, Paul looked up toward the church tower. A light flickered and then shone steadily. It was immediately followed by a second.

Lying in the river ahead of them was the British frigate *Somerset,* stationed there in midstream on this night of April 18th, to keep men like Paul Revere from leaving Boston. Her bulk loomed big and black, studded with riding lights. But the skiff glided silently past her stern with not a sound of alarm from on board. A few minutes later, Paul stepped ashore in Charlestown.

A group of men were waiting for him at Colonel Conant's house.

"Welcome, Paul," the colonel said. "We received your signal."

"And you have a horse for me?"

"The finest horse in Charlestown. Deacon Larkin's chestnut."

"Good. Then I'll be riding."

"A word of caution, Paul. British mounted patrols have been out on all the roads since early afternoon. Keep an eye skinned for them."

Paul stepped into the saddle and patted the chestnut on its gleaming neck.

So into the moonlit night rode Paul Revere

"I'll venture that a good Yankee horse can out-run 'em," he said.

He touched his spurs to the animal's sides, and in an instant horse and rider were swallowed up by the shadows.

So into the moonlit night rode Paul Revere. He gave his mount its head as they galloped through sleeping Charlestown and out across the neck of land that led from that village to Cambridge. The rhythmic motion of the horse felt good. He eased back in the saddle for the long ride.

Suddenly two mounted figures rode out of the shadow of a grove of trees into the clear moonlight of the road. They were so close that Paul could see the British cockades on their hats and the moonbeams glancing off the polished butts of their holstered pistols.

"Halt!"

Paul wheeled the chestnut around on a shilling piece and struck out across the open country at a dead run. In this rough going, the heavy British chargers were no match for the fleet-footed Yankee horse. Paul glanced back over his shoulder just in time to see the leading horse stumble into a clay bog. There was no sign of the second rider. He patted his horse on the neck, and they raced on.

They struck the Mystick Road, pounded over the plank bridge that crossed the river and into Medford Town. At the home of the captain of the Medford Minute Men, Paul skidded the chestnut to a stop, leaped from his saddle, and pounded on the door.

A sleepy head poked out from an upper window.

"Stop making all that noise down there!"

"Noise!" Paul shouted back. "You'll have enough noise to suit you before morning! The British Regulars are coming out!"

Then he vaulted into the saddle and was off again.

At every farmhouse along the Lexington high-road Paul Revere stopped long enough to shout his warning:

"Wake up! The Regulars are out!"

The village clock was sounding the last stroke of midnight when the flying hoofs of the Yankee horse thundered into Lexington.

Rob Gordon was awakened by a noisy commotion in the public room down below, and the loud, discordant rumble of a dozen men talking at once. He yawned, stretched, and prepared to roll over and go back to sleep when he heard the name, *Paul Revere.*

He cocked an ear. Then he caught fragments of conversation that floated up out of the hubbub:

". . . when d'ye think they'll get here, Paul . . . ?"

". . . how many you reckon are comin' . . . ?"

". . . better start ringin' the church-bells . . ."

". . . now, hold on a minute, Jeb . . ."

Rob bounced out of bed like a rubber ball, all thought of sleep jolted out of his head. He slipped on his shoes and hustled down the stairs.

Paul Revere was standing at the service bar, the center of a milling group of excited, loud-talking men. Despite the chill of the night, his face was flushed and sweat-streaked from the exertion and excitement of his ride.

"So you have seen nought of Billy Dawes?" he was saying as Rob entered the room. "He had the start of nigh an hour on me. But then he was to take the long way, around the Neck. Likely he had trouble with the guard at the gate. Old Gage has clamped down—"

He was interrupted by the sound of a galloping

[*70*]

horse on the road outside, and the pawing and scuffling of its hoofs as the rider pulled it to an abrupt stop. Then there were sounds of heavy boots tramping across the porch, and a tall, thin young man burst through the door.

"Billy!" Paul Revere shouted. "We were just discussing you, man. We feared a Redcoat patrol had nabbed you."

Rob had heard many stories about Billy Dawes, but until now he had never laid eyes on the man who, next to Paul Revere, was the most famous horseman and express rider in the colony. His nose was long, as was his chin, and his eyes, set close together under bushy brows, twinkled in perpetual merriment.

"Nab me they didn't," he grinned. "But make a liar out of me they did. I told 'em my sweetheart in Roxbury Town would have no more to do with me if I failed to keep my promise to call on her tonight. So after 'most an hour of joshing me, one poor romantic soul, thinkin' no doubt of the gal he left behind in County Kent, opened up the gate and let me pass. And here I am."

At this story, there was a raucous chorus of guffaws, and over the melee rose the voice of Paul Revere:

"If good Mistress Dawes learns of this sweetheart of yours in Roxbury, Billy, a fight with the British will seem like child's play. And now drink down a hot cup of Mr. Buckman's tea, for as soon as our horses have caught their second wind, we must ride on to Concord."

A young man standing at the bar spoke up. Rob recognized him as Sam Prescott, a doctor just out of Harvard College, who lived in Concord.

"I'll ride with you. They say that British cavalry patrols are as thick tonight as ants around an ant-hill. I'll welcome the company."

"Good," said Paul Revere. "We'll leave in half an hour."

As Rob listened to the furious gabble of talk that flowed back and forth across the room, he could feel a tingle through all his nerves that sent the blood pounding at his heart and throbbing in his temples. He elbowed his way through the crowd to stand beside Paul Revere.

"Mr. Revere, sir."

Paul Revere turned round at the sound of Rob's voice. He was a good head shorter than the tall, gangling boy, and he had to raise his eyes slightly when he spoke.

"Well, now," he smiled, "it's young Rob Gordon. I heard tell in Boston of your ruckus with the Redcoats last night. That was good work."

"May I ride with you to Concord, sir? If the British patrols are out, as Dr. Prescott says, somebody might get caught. With another rider there'd be a better chance of at least one man getting through."

Paul stroked his square-cut jaw.

"The patrols are out, right enough. I ran smack into one near Medford and got away by the skin of my horse's hind hoof."

"My old Roman Nose is the fastest horse in Lexington," Rob begged. "You can ask anyone."

"That's so," a militia man volunteered.

"Whoa up, lad!" John Buckman shook his head and held up his hand, palm outward, in a gesture that plainly said no. "This is man's work tonight."

Paul Revere grinned at the tavern keeper.

"There's one Britisher nursing an aching head in Boston tonight, John, who could tell you that this lad is more man than he could handle. Let the boy come with us. We can make use of an extra rider."

Rob didn't wait for John Buckman's answer. He flew through the back door toward the stable to saddle old Roman Nose.

[*73*]

CHAPTER SIX

Ambush!

THE bells in the steeple of Lexington's church house were ringing out their warning as Paul Revere, Billy Dawes, Sam Prescott, and Rob Gordon galloped past the Green and out onto the hard-packed dirt of the highroad to Concord. They rode two abreast, Rob and Dr. Prescott bringing up the rear. At every farmhouse, one of them turned aside to alert the family and then galloped furiously to catch up with his companions.

Halfway to Concord, a lane turned off the highroad to the right and meandered through a meadow to a house and a group of farm buildings on a knoll.

"That's Mr. Hartwell's place," Rob called. "I'll

go." He pulled Roman Nose's head around and cantered toward the house.

Like most of the other farmers near to town, Mr. Hartwell had already been awakened by the clanging of the Lexington bells. At Rob's shout, he stepped out from the candlelit front room of the house onto the small porch. His nightshirt was tucked into his breeches, and he held a musket dangling in his hand. His family was crowded around the doorway behind him.

"It's Rob Gordon, sir! The British Regulars are marching from Cambridge!"

"When d'ye expect they'll get here, son?"

"No telling, sir. Paul Revere says they started out of Boston about ten o'clock. Likely they'll be in Lexington well before daylight. Cap'n Parker says to melt down all your lead into balls and get to Buckman's as fast as you can."

"Lead's all melted down, son," the farmer said. "Womenfolks took care of that yesterday. Thankee, son, for the warnin'."

Rob wheeled the dancing Roman Nose and dashed back out the lane and down the road. Two hundred yards ahead, he could make out his friends cantering along in the clear moonlight.

[75]

He put Roman Nose into a gallop and was just about to shout at them when the crack of a pistol shot shattered the stillness of the night.

At the same instant, he saw two British officers knee their horses out of the shadow of a clump of trees and ride out directly into the path of the three Yankees.

"Halt! One inch farther and ye're all dead men!"

Rob could hear their voices distinctly in the crisp, quiet air.

Three other British horsemen appeared out of the darkness. Then two more. And then things happened so furiously that all the separate pieces of the picture fused into a jumbled blur before Rob's horrified eyes.

Sam Prescott yelled: "Put on!" and slashed at the nearest Britisher with the butt of his riding crop, then raced for a high stone wall at the right of the road.

Paul Revere wheeled his chestnut to the left, toward a patch of woods. As he did so, six Red-

coat cavalrymen emerged from the wood's shadows, three on either side, and closed in on him. They grabbed his horse's bridle and skidded him to a stop.

"I've got two of 'em, boys!" That was the voice of the lanky Billy Dawes. As he yelled, Dawes put his big gray stallion at the two troopers who were blocking the road ahead. The startled Redcoats gave ground, but the gray stallion lost his footing and went to his knees. Billy shot from the saddle over the horse's head like a stone thrown from a sling. He rolled over twice, landed on his feet running, and disappeared into the trees.

Out of the corner of an eye, Rob could see Paul Revere, dismounted, standing between two cavalrymen. Each held a pistol at his head. At the same time, Rob saw Sam Prescott's horse clear the stone wall and gallop furiously across a farmer's pasture field, the doctor bending low over the horse's neck. A pistol flamed and cracked. Then another. Sam Prescott raced on and disappeared over the top of a rise.

Scarcely ten seconds had gone by since the first warning shot. Rob pulled Roman Nose to a quick stop, trying in all the confusion to make up

[78]

his mind what to do, when he heard the hammering of horses' hoofs coming up on his right.

"Here's another one! Halt, there!"

The moonlight revealed still another pair of British horsemen bearing down on him.

Rob looked around wildly. There was no escape on either side. He kicked Roman Nose savagely in the ribs, and the big horse leaped forward. Down the road the British patrol had spread out, and there was an open way to the stone wall over which Sam Prescott had fled. Rob put the bay full at it.

There was another yell from behind him, and what sounded like an angry hornet whistled past his ear, followed instantly by a pistol's sharp crack. Then the wall loomed up in front of him. In the moonlit darkness it looked as high as a house. Rob leaned forward over the pommel, his face whipped by Roman Nose's flying mane, his hands low on either side of the horse's head, holding the reins up short. One stride away from the wall, he gave the bay a lusty kick and lifted up his head. Old Roman Nose tucked his front legs under him, took off with a powerful, up-thrusting jump, and soared over the wall like a homesick pigeon.

[79]

Another pistol cracked behind him, and then Rob, too, was pounding across the pasture field.

A quarter of a mile farther on, he came to the road again. He put Roman Nose over another wall, and then gave him his head as they raced on toward Concord.

This time he didn't stop to alarm individual farmhouses. Sam Prescott appeared to have gotten away safely, but there was no way Rob could be sure. For all he knew, he was the only messenger left to carry the news of the coming attack, and the countryside might be swarming with patrols like the one he had just escaped from. He couldn't afford to lose time! He had to make it through!

CHAPTER SEVEN

The Minute Men

THE Concord churchbells had taken up the insistent pealing of the distant bells in Lexington as Rob raced into the town square. The moon was setting and the night was turning black. But lights burned in every house, and Rob could see the shadowy forms of men milling around on the village Green in the glow of soft candlelight that streamed out the open door of Wright's Tavern.

He pulled up in front of the tavern's hitching rail and slipped from the saddle. Small clouds of steam rose from old Roman Nose's sweating flanks and withers, the result of having covered the last three miles from the ambush below Mr. Hartwell's farm at a dead run. Standing hip-shot at the rail was Dr. Prescott's black stallion. So the doctor had

[*81*]

made it! Rob looped his reins over the bar and went inside.

Sam Prescott was in the center of a group of excited men. The tall man who was doing most of the talking, Rob knew, was Colonel James Barrett, commanding officer of the Concord Minute Men. The companies from the various towns around had called themselves by this name because, as they liked to boast, they were ready to leave their farms and "fight at a minute's notice."

The young doctor looked up as Rob came into the room, a big smile creasing his dirt-streaked face.

"Rob, lad! I feared the Redcoats had nabbed you for sure!" He turned to Colonel Barrett. "This is the boy who rode with us from Lexington." Then, to Rob, "How did the others fare?"

"I saw them capture Mr. Revere," Rob replied. "And Mr. Dawes, too, I think. Leastwise, he was thrown from his horse. Roman Nose and I showed them our heels by taking the same wall you did."

Sam Prescott gave his head a worried shake. "I fear it will go hard with Paul. The British have had him in their black books for a long while. He can call himself lucky if he escapes a hangman's noose for this night's work."

"And we can call ourselves lucky," Colonel Barrett commented drily, "that he got as far as Lexington with his warning. Nigh two hundred men have reported in already, and a dozen riders are out on the roads alarming the outlying farms."

Sam Prescott drained off the last dregs of a steaming mug which he held in his hand.

"And I had best be off to carry your message to the men at Acton," he said. "My horse should have his second wind by now, not that the big brute needs it much."

Colonel Barrett's lined face softened into the nearest thing to a grin that he was able to manage.

"I was right unhappy when you refused to sell me that black last winter," he said. "Now I'm glad you didn't."

Dr. Prescott fastened the collar of his long riding cloak around his neck and settled his three-cornered hat firmly on his head.

"How long, sir, d'ye think it will take the column to get here?" he asked.

The colonel glanced at a tall grandfather's clock which stood in a corner of the room.

"It's close on to two. If, as you say, the British left Boston at ten last night, and assuming they march light and fast, as I think they will, they should be approaching Lexington in an hour. Say two at most. So you'd best tell Captain Davis at Acton to get his men here on the double."

"Right, sir." Sam Prescott laid his hand on Rob's shoulder as he turned to go.

"Good work, lad."

Then he went out the doorway and disappeared into the night. In a few moments, the flying hoof-beats of his stallion faded down the road.

Rob turned to Colonel Barrett.

"Sir, I'm ready to ride anywhere you want to send me."

"Fine, boy, fine! But for the moment, you'd best see to your horse and then hold yourself in readiness. I'll send for you if I need you."

Rob went outside, untied Roman Nose from the hitching rail, and led him slowly down the road to the stable next to Brown's saddlery. There he rubbed him briskly with handfuls of hay, loosened the saddle girth, forked a bit of fresh hay down from the loft for him to nibble on, and returned to the Green.

[*84*]

The number of Minute Men in the town seemed to have nearly doubled since he had entered the tavern a short while before. Some sat on the ground with their backs against trees and dozed, their muskets held upright between their knees. Others gathered in small groups around the town meeting house, or tried to crowd into the already overflowing public room of Wright's Tavern. No one spoke loudly, but a hum of jumbled talk and muffled conversation hung over the Green like the constant sound of buzzing that hovers over a beehive.

Rob recognized farmers and townspeople from Lincoln, Bedford, Chelmsford, Weston, and half a dozen other nearby towns. Here and there, men were greasing their muskets or checking their loads. A few had old-fashioned powder horns slung over their shoulders, but most carried the more modern cartridge boxes. Some were bare-headed, others wore black three-cornered hats, while still others wore the shapeless, flopping felt hats affected by Yankee farmers.

Every few minutes another company straggled in to swell the makeshift army, the men slouching along in uneven lines. Rob had never seen so many people gathered together in one place in all his life. The Redcoats were going to get a surprise when they came marching into Concord! There was no mistake about that!

He sauntered into the tavern and found an empty seat in a corner. Before he knew it, the excitement and weariness of the past two days had caught up with him, and he dozed off into a fitful sleep.

He was awakened by a hand roughly shaking his shoulder.

"Wake up, boy! The colonel's been lookin' all over for you."

Rob jumped to his feet. The hands of the clock in the corner were creeping upwards toward four. He found Colonel Barrett seated at a table before a roaring fire.

"You wanted me, sir?"

The colonel was all business.

"Your horse is ready to travel?"

"Yes, sir."

"Then look you, boy. There's been no word of the British column. Ride toward Lexington and see if you can find any sign of 'em. Keep an eye peeled for mounted patrols, and hightail it back here the instant you have anything to report."

His keen eyes bored into Rob's.

"Remember, son. No jackanapes! Get back here quick, as soon as you catch sight of 'em."

"Yes, *sir!*"

Rob dashed from the inn, ran down the street to the stable, and led out Roman Nose. In minutes

he was pounding down the Lexington road the way he had come two hours before.

As he cantered cautiously past the fork in the road below the Hartwell place, he saw no sign of the British patrol that had been waiting in ambush earlier. But he did notice that the first faint streaks of daylight were beginning to paint the sky a pale pink in the direction of Boston. By the time he turned into the yard at Buckman's, the day was noticeably brightening.

The Lexington Minute Company, about a hundred strong, Rob reckoned, was lined up on the Green, most of the men leaning casually on their muskets. Captain Parker walked up and down in front of them, quietly giving orders. Nearly half as many more men were crowded inside the tavern. As Rob came through the door an argument seemed to be going on. It centered around the short, stocky redheaded person of Mutt Cooper, the little cockney who was drill-master of the Lexington company.

Rob knew Mutt Cooper well. One day last winter, wearing the mud-stained remnants of a British uniform, he had trudged into town and announced himself as a deserter from General Gage's army. He proved to be an excellent horse-shoer and iron-worker, and soon had steady employment in Mr. Dillard's blacksmith shop. Once a mounted Redcoat patrol had come out from Boston looking for him, but Mutt had hidden in the belfry of the church until they were gone.

Then, one Sunday afternoon, he was taking his ease on Buckman's front steps and watching the men of the Minute Company struggle awkwardly through the manual of arms. At first he had grinned tolerantly at the clumsiness of these farmer-soldiers. Then, finally, when his professional pride could stand it no longer, he had stepped out onto the Green and taken a man's musket from his hands.

" 'Ere," he said. "Hi'll show ye 'ow a proper sojer does hit!"

Whereupon he had snapped through the drill with the smart precision of a British Regular.

From that moment, by common consent, Mutt had taken over as drillmaster. And if the Lexington company still fell short of the standards of a platoon from the crack Royal Welsh Fusiliers, it still made a better showing on the drill ground than did most companies from the towns around.

Now, Mutt's face was redder than usual as the argument went on around him.

"See here, Cooper," John Buckman was saying, "it's right and proper enough for you to leave the King's army if you were a mind to. And to come here and teach our men how to handle their weapons as well. But there's no call for you to stand out there with a loaded musket and fire on your own countrymen."

"They're no countrymen o' mine!" the cockney roared, his voice as high and shrill as the crow of any gamecock. "Hi am a proper Yankee now, Hi am, same as th' rest o' ye. An' Hi claims th' right to stand an' fight alongside o' th' comp'ny Hi've been drillin'."

"He's right, John!" a man yelled over the din. "He's just as much a Minute Man as any of the rest of us!"

Rob's entrance broke up the argument as the men crowded around him for news. Briefly he told them what had happened since he had left Lexington with the other three riders. There was much muttering, clucking of tongues, and shaking of heads when he related the details of Paul Revere's capture.

"But it's news that *I've* come for," he said to John Buckman. "Have you had any word of the British, Uncle John?"

John Buckman shook his head. "None, lad, and that's a mystery. We sent out two scouts not an hour ago, but neither one of 'em has returned.

Cap'n Parker has been waiting for full daylight to send others after them."

"It's well nigh daylight now," Rob said. "Colonel Barrett ordered me to scout the column, so I'd best ride down the road and have a look."

"Hi'll go with ye, lad," Mutt Cooper said, separating himself from the crowd. "Hi'd like to get a good look-see at me late comrades-in-harms."

Outside, the little cockney said:

"We'd best leave yer 'orse, lad, and go it on foot. Hi've a funny feelin' in me bones that th' captain's scouts rode square into th' bloody British column and got theirselves took 'fore they knew wot 'appened to 'em. We'll keep to th' ridges an' stay out o' sight."

As he walked quickly across the yard at Mutt Cooper's side, Rob heard a noise in the shrubbery at the corner of the inn, and a small voice:

"Rob!"

Sary ran from her hiding place and came up to him.

"I've been watching from the window upstairs, Rob, and I saw you ride up."

She grasped his arm and clung to it.

"Are the British really on their way to Lexington?"

"I'm afraid they are, Sary," Rob told her. "Mr. Cooper and I are going out to scout them now. So you had best get safe back in your room."

He turned and started to walk away. Sary followed.

"I'm coming with you, Rob."

Rob stopped again, a frown darkening his face.

"Now, see here, Sary. We're likely heading into a fight. That's no place for a girl. Go back now, before I pick you up and carry you."

Sary's temper flared.

"You just try it, Mr. Rob Gordon! I've been cooped up in my room all night, hearing all those goings-on downstairs and not knowing what they're about. If you think you can carry me back, you just try it!"

Rob advanced toward her with both arms outstretched. "All right," he said. "I will."

" 'Ere, 'ere," Mutt Cooper laughed. "We're headin' for no fight. Not just now, we ain't. Let th' lass come along. But mind," he said to Sary, "that ye keep quiet, missy."

Walking swiftly, they cut across the Green and up to the top of a high ridge that paralleled the highroad to Boston. They walked along it, through newly plowed fields and patches of woods, for nearly a mile. Then suddenly, as they topped a gentle rise, they looked down into the little valley and saw the whole British army spread out in a long, winding column below them.

"Duck!" Mutt Cooper ordered, and the three crouched in the shelter of a stone wall.

Peering up over the wall, Rob and Sary watched wide-eyed as the column flowed along the narrow road between bordering stone walls like a loose-jointed, undulating snake. The shining steel of polished bayonets reflected the pale rays of the morning sun. The long uniform coats of the marching men gleamed brilliant crimson, and their white crossbelts shone. But Rob noticed that every soldier was plastered with mud from the waist down, as though the army had struggled through a swamp. Likely, he thought, they'd got bogged down when they disembarked from their boats in the Cambridge marshes. That would account for the fact that they were so far behind schedule.

Two officers, one very fat and the other slim and tall in the saddle, rode in the lead.

"That's Leftenant Colonel Francis Smith, the fat 'un," Mutt whispered. "'E'd be in command. Tother one's Major John Pitcairn o' th' Royal

*They saw the whole British army spread out in a long,
winding column below them*

Marines. Bloody best sojer in Boston, 'e is. Th' Marines is right be'ind 'im, leadin' th' column.''

There must have been seven or eight hundred men in the column all told, Rob figured. It stretched out, the men marching four abreast, clean down around a turn and out of sight. The ranks were orderly, and non-commissioned officers ran up and down the road, keeping the lines smartly dressed and the companies closed up.

Mutt pointed out the different units as the army wound along the road.

"There's th' King's Own Reg'ment comin' right after th' Marines, the ones wi' th' blue facin's on their coats. And right be'ind is the South Staffordshires. Then followin' them is th' Royal Welsh. And next is—''

"Look yonder!'' Rob grabbed Mutt by the arm. "There's Cap'n Parker's scouts, or I'm an Injun!''

Two men in the dark homespun clothes of Yankee farmers trudged along at the side of the column, their bare heads bent and their hands tied securely behind them.

"Ye're no Injun, boy! Them's th' cap'n's scouts an' no mistake. Rode right smack into th' column in th' dark and got theirselves took, just like Hi said. Good job we stuck to th' heights!''

Sary hadn't said a word since they sighted the column, but Rob could feel a shiver run through her as she huddled close beside him. He put his arm around her shoulder and squeezed her reassuringly.

"Don't be frightened, Sary honey."

"I—I just can't help it, Rob." Her teeth were chattering, and not alone, Rob knew, from the early morning chill. "It—it's so—so *scary!* All those soldiers down there coming right into Lexington!"

Mutt Cooper tugged at Rob's sleeve.

"Let's be goin', lad. We've seen about all we came t' see."

Crouching still, they backed away from the wall and behind the sheltering top of the hill.

"Now," Mutt said, straightening up, "we'd best get back to Buckman's fast!"

He started off at a dog-trot, and Rob and Sary, holding hands, followed close behind him.

"Redcoats!" Rob yelled as they ran across the Green to the tavern door. "The Redcoats are half a mile down the road!"

Instantly, a drummer boy standing at Captain Parker's side began beating out a sharp, rolling *rat-ta-tat—tat,tat,tat!* on his drum, and the lounging Minute Men snapped to attention and formed into a ragged line. Two dozen others, hearing the shouts and the beating of the drum, streamed out of the tavern and joined them. Mutt Cooper dashed across the Green to the blacksmith shop and reappeared a minute later with a musket in his hand. He was loading it as he ran.

For the next few minutes, all was confusion. Rob took Sary around the house to the kitchen door.

"There's bound to be some shooting, Sary," he said. "You and your ma best get upstairs and stay away from the windows. I've got to ride back to Concord and take the word to the colonel."

Sary squeezed Rob's hand, onto which she had been holding tightly ever since they had run from the ridge.

"Be careful, Rob! Oh, *please* be careful!"

Rob's heart was pounding so hard in his throat that he could hardly keep his voice even enough to speak. He took a deep breath to calm himself for a second.

"Don't worry about me, Sary honey. You just go take care of your ma."

He turned and raced for the hitching rack where he had left Roman Nose.

[*97*]

The excitement going on all around him had made the big bay nervous and skittish. When Rob came up to him, he pawed in the dirt with his off front hoof and nickered shrilly, both ears laid flat back against his head.

"Easy, now!" Rob said, stroking his long, silky forelock.

The boy stood there for a moment watching, fascinated, the scene that was unfolding before his eyes. The Lexington Minute Company stood in a long double line, almost squarely in the middle of the Green. Some of the men were loading and priming their pieces. Others held their muskets at the ready in front of them, as a hunter does when he is waiting for a partridge to flush from cover.

Rob noticed that a number of the men, maybe two dozen in all, had stepped away from the line on the Green and were taking up positions behind stone walls on the left side of the road. A second group of some forty or fifty, all armed, stood around the meeting house, apparently undecided as to whether they should join the Minute Company's line or seek shelter behind the walls.

Captain John Parker strode up and down in

front of the company line, his sword drawn.

"Cap'n!" Rob recognized the voice of Mutt Cooper, speaking up from the front rank.

"Cap'n, ye think we should stand right 'ere an' meet 'em square? Oughtn't we all get be'ind th' walls and take 'em on th' flank?"

"No!" Captain Parker's voice thundered over the noise. "Boys," he said, "stand your ground! Don't fire unless you're fired on! But if they mean to have war, let it begin here!"

A hush fell over the assembled men. Out of the corner of his eye, Rob could make out the first glint of morning sunlight striking British bayonets as the column approached, now only two hundred yards from the Lexington Green.

He vaulted into the saddle, pulled Roman Nose's head around sharply, and galloped across the Green and up the slope to the Concord road.

Before he was out of earshot, he heard the hollow report of a musket behind him. It was followed by another, and then a third.

And then a ragged volley of shots ripped the still morning air. They echoed up the narrow valley and over the hilltops, and seemed to lend wings to his horse's flying feet.

[*99*]

CHAPTER EIGHT

The Battle Green

SARY WILLIAMS stood peeking out the open window of her upstairs bedroom. From it, she had a clear view of the Green spread out below, and the ragged line of Minute Men that stretched across its middle. There was much yelling and shouting. The men of Captain Parker's company stood firmly in their places, but almost as many others ran aimlessly back and forth between the meeting house and the stone walls that edged the Green.

"Sary! Sary!" It was her mother's voice, shaking with fear and dread, calling from another room. "Get away from that window, Sary, and come in here with me!"

But the bustling excitement of the scene down

below held Sary spellbound, as the sight of a snake's flickering tongue charms a bird into stony stillness.

"Sary!" The second sharp call from her mother broke the spell, and she started to turn away. Just then a mounted British officer, the one Mutt Cooper had said was Major Pitcairn, came into view from between the rows of houses that hid the Boston road. He was riding a coal-black charger. Behind him, marching smartly in close ranks, was the regiment of Royal Marines. Without hesitating, the major marched his men onto the grass of the Green, straight at the line of waiting Minute Men.

Twenty yards from the Rebel muskets, Major Pitcairn threw his right arm up above his head.

"Halt!"

The moving column stopped in its tracks.

"Pre—sent *arms!*"

Sary could hear the command clearly in the sudden silence that had settled over the Green like a blanket.

There was a clatter of hands slapping against musket butts as the red-coated soldiers shifted their guns from their shoulders into firing position. The major drew a sword from his belt and pointed it straight at Captain Parker.

"Ye're Rebels!" Every word came clear to Sary's ears. "Disperse! Lay down yer arms!"

There was a stir through the Minute Company. The men looked at each other, then at Captain Parker, undecided whether or not to fire. By this time, more British soldiers had marched onto the Green, until their scarlet coats and black bear-skin hats seemed to fill half of it completely.

"Lay down yer arms, blast ye, and disperse!" Major Pitcairn's voice roared. "If ye don't lay down yer arms, ye're all dead men!"

There was another moment of breath-taking silence. Sary stood frozen, her mouth open.

She saw Captain Parker look out over the British army, as though comparing its strength with his own. Then through the open window, she heard his voice rise above the stillness:

"Fall out, men! Every man take care of himself!"

At that, the line of the Minute Company began to disintegrate, as each man turned to leave the Green or stood wondering what his next move should be.

The British major's voice rang out:

"Right—ob-*lique!*"

The Redcoat column moved again, swerving to the right to march past and surround the Rebel line.

At that instant there was a puff of smoke from behind a stone wall at the edge of the Green, and the dull boom of a musket. Major Pitcairn's horse reared and fell on its side. The first shot was followed by another, and then a third. A British soldier in the front rank staggered and pitched forward. The major had leaped from the saddle as his horse went down, but the animal instantly scrambled to its feet, apparently not badly hurt by the musket ball that had struck it.

Now a volley of musket fire ripped out from the line of British infantrymen. As if by a miracle, none of the Minute Men fell. Then some of the Rebels began returning the fire. And before Sary's horror-stricken eyes, muskets started cracking from all parts of the Green. A haze of blue-black powder smoke rose like a cloud into the air.

By now, most of the Minute Men were running for safety, British soldiers pursuing them and firing as they ran. Sary saw one man shoot at the British line and then stop to reload his gun. As he did so, a Redcoat fired at him point-blank. The man's knees buckled. As he was going down, the Britisher buried his bayonet in his throat. Another Minute Man, running across the Green, stumbled as though he had tripped over a root, threw his musket into the air as he went down, and fell forward head over heels. Right below her window, a man sprinted for the shelter of the tavern door. As he approached the steps, he lurched forward as though he had been struck a sharp blow on the back. He went to his knees, struggled back on his feet, staggered to the tavern porch, and collapsed in a heap.

The British soldiers were yelling and shouting as they fired, seemingly for the moment out of control. Major Pitcairn was back in the saddle, and again he was swinging his sword. But now he was beating it against the muskets and over the heads and shoulders of his own men, and Sary could hear his voice shouting shrilly over the din:

"Cease fire! Cease fire! Keep yer ranks and surround 'em!"

At the same instant, another yell from the disordered British ranks jerked Sary's eyes to another part of the Green.

Major Pitcairn was back in the saddle

"Burn the place! Kill the Rebels and burn the town!"

She shrank back against the wall beside the window as a group of Redcoats broke from the column and rushed toward the tavern.

"Burn the inn! Burn the Rebels out!"

A young officer dashed up to the tavern steps swinging his sword over his head.

"Back into the ranks, blast ye! Back into the ranks!"

The soldiers stopped, looked around sheepishly, and then melted once again into the red-coated throng.

The young officer glanced at the wounded man who lay on the steps. Then he, too, turned and was swallowed up by the milling mob of soldiers.

Then, as abruptly as it had started, the firing stopped. The last of the Minute Men had disappeared from the Green and faded into the protection of the stone walls or behind the houses. Some of them were racing up the sides of the hill above the Bedford road and over the ridge. Eight still, brown-coated heaps dotted the emerald grass of the Green. Here and there, a man too badly wounded to walk, was crawling away on his hands and knees. Captain Parker stood alone where he had formed the Minute Company line, his sword drooping from his hand, its lowered point touching the ground.

The British column had re-formed itself, and once again it was moving precisely across the Green, past the meeting house, and up the slope at the far end toward the narrow ribbon of road that led to Concord. A skirl of fifes and rattle of drums beat out time for the tramping feet.

Sary shook herself out of the half-daze that the sudden noise and tumult of the battle had brought upon her. She ran from the room and down the stairs.

As she emerged from the tavern's public room and into the outdoors, her nose was stung by the acrid fumes of powder smoke that still hung suspended in the cool morning air. Two dozen men who had watched the short fight from inside the tavern were milling about on the porch.

Sary dropped to her knees and bent over the wounded man she had seen collapse on the steps. She'd seen him in the tavern many times. He was John Mason, a farmer from over Bedford way. A bright red, sticky mass of blood spread in a widening stain over the right shoulder of his brown shirt. She rolled him over gently, until his head rested in her lap.

John Mason opened his eyes and looked up into hers.

"Rum," he said faintly. "Get—rum."

A man standing behind her heard the request.

"I'll get it, missy." He dashed into the tavern and returned a moment later with a brown bottle in his hand. He gave it to Sary, and she held the bottle to the man's lips.

John Mason shook his head weakly.

"No—no. Wash the wound—with rum."

From the pocket of her skirt, Sary took a small pair of sewing scissors which she always carried there. With swift movements, she cut the shirt from the man's back. There was a jagged, blood-crusted hole high on the muscles of his chest where the British ball had come out.

She soaked a piece of the shirt in rum and swabbed gently at the ragged wound. John Mason gritted his teeth and squinted his eyes tight shut when the stinging liquid bit into the raw and bleeding flesh.

"That's—the stuff—missy," he said. But his lips quivered with pain.

Sary washed the wound, both front and back, with the burning, stinging rum. Then, reaching the scissors up under her skirt, she cut the bottom from her linen petticoat. With the clean strip of cloth she bandaged the wound tightly.

When she was finished, John Mason let his head rest for another moment in her lap. Tiny beads of ice-cold perspiration stood out on his pale forehead and underneath his eyes.

Then he managed a weak smile.

"I—I think I can make it now."

He placed his hands on the boards of the porch floor and tried to push himself up. The man who had brought the bottle of rum from the tavern put a hand under his good shoulder and helped him to his feet. John Mason's fingers reached out and touched Sary on the sleeve.

"Thanks, missy! Thank ye kindly!"

Then he turned to the man who was supporting him.

"I think I can use some rum now tother way—with the good landlord's butter and hot spice."

The two disappeared through the tavern's open door.

Sary's hands were shaking as she got to her feet. Then she saw a short figure of a man staggering toward the steps. It was the cockney drillmaster, Mutt Cooper. A red slash above his right eye dripped a bright rivulet of blood down over his face.

Sary ran to him, took him by the arm, and helped him to the porch. She sat him down, then turned to the rum bottle and soaked another piece of cloth in the golden-brown liquid. She swabbed at the gash, and Mutt Cooper jerked his head back sharply and yelled.

"There, there," Sary said soothingly. "I know it stings, but it's good for you."

Just why raw rum, applied to the torn flesh of an open wound, was good for it, Sary had no idea. But it had appeared to help Mr. Mason, and so it should help Mr. Cooper. She soaked the cloth again and washed the blood from the little Englishman's face.

This time, he grinned through clenched teeth.

"Hit looks like a Redcoat musket ball creased me 'ead, in a manner o' speakin'. Glanced off me thick skull, it did, no doubt. But th' rum do seem to 'elp, for a' that. Never knew there was more 'n one use for th' stuff."

With her scissors, Sary cut another bandage from her petticoat hem and wrapped it around his head.

"Gracious," she thought, "at this rate I soon won't have any petticoat left!"

Mutt got to his feet. The stinging of the rum seemed to have cleared his head and brightened his eyes. He looked around for his musket, and picked it up from the steps where it had dropped.

[*111*]

"Ye're an angel o' mercy, Miss Sary. Now Hi think Hi'd best be off over th' 'ills for Concord Town. Hi've a bit of a score to settle with Mister Gen'ral Gage and me late Redcoat friends."

He slung the musket over his shoulder, barrel first, and strode off across the Green in the direction of the low hills that led to Concord.

"Sary! Sary! Look here, girl!"

Sary wheeled around. John Buckman stood with two other men who were supporting a wounded Yankee. The man's face was pale, and his arms dangled limply at his sides.

"Come over here, Sary," John Buckman said, "and see if you can do anything for poor Worthe Faulkner. He's bad hurt."

The whole front of Worthe Faulkner's homespun shirt was a sodden mass of oozing blood.

Sary shut her eyes tight for a moment, and her head spun round and round. Then she opened her eyes, and her chin jutted out defiantly.

She took the scissors from her pocket.

"Here," she ordered, "hold his shirt away from him while I cut it off his back."

One of the men hastened to do as she said.

Grimly, her heart sick, Sary set to work.

CHAPTER NINE

The Music March

ROB GORDON reined in his sweating horse before Colonel Barrett, Major Buttrick, Captain Brown, and a dozen other officers of the Minute Men gathered together in a tight group on Concord Green. It was full daylight now, and the sun glistened on the dew-wet leaves of the oaks and elms and maples that fringed the square as Rob slid from Roman Nose's back.

"They're in Lexington, sir," he reported. "And likely headed this way by now."

Rob told the officers of the scout which he, Sary, and Mutt Cooper had made, of the stand that Captain Parker had intended to take on Lexington Green, and of the firing he had heard as he rode out of town.

[*113*]

"They're in Lexington, sir," he reported

"I don't see how the Lexington Company can hold 'em very long, sir. Mr. Cooper and I calc'lated that the British force is nigh eight hundred strong. And Cap'n Parker's company is likely no more than a hundred."

"They'll be comin' on," Colonel Barrett said drily. "No doubt of that." He looked out over the swarm of Minute Men that had been drifting into town since the early hours of the morning. "Well, we've got a fair number here. I'm thinkin' we can give 'em a fight."

He began issuing orders to the company commanders who stood around him.

"Jamie, take your company to the high ground on tother side of the river.

"Will, you and your men go with him. Spread out along the walls on the far side of the bridge.

"Joe—Nat—Jake—George—all of you get over the river and place your companies along the ridge on either side of Jamie and Will. When we come at 'em, we want to come at 'em for all we're worth."

A strident voice rose up over the colonel's crisp, businesslike commands.

"Hey—Jim!"

It was Amos Barrett, a young cousin of the colonel.

"Hey, Jim! Me and Cap'n Dave Brown have got us an idea."

Colonel Barrett twisted around, his face suddenly gone red. He spotted the speaker and wagged a finger at him.

"Amos," he said sternly, "this is a military organization, and I'm yer commanding officer. I'll thank you to address me in the future as Colonel."

"Why, I'm right sorry, Jim—I mean Colonel. But me and Dave figure that one Yankee, fightin' Injun style, ought to be worth two or three Lobsterbacks. We aim to take our companies down th' road to meet 'em."

"Nonsense, Amos!" the colonel roared. "Ye're daft! Get yer men back over yonder on the far ridge with—"

"Wait a minute, Colonel." It was Seth Greene, captain of one of the Concord companies. "Why not let the crazy galoots try it? Could be a show of force like that might scare th' Redcoats off."

The colonel took off his three-cornered hat and scratched his gray head as he allowed this notion to sink in. Then a thin smile cut across his lean face.

"Go to it then, Amos," he said at last. "But watch yer step. Don't try to stand agin' 'em if they show fight."

This was something Rob didn't want to miss! Swiftly, he led Roman Nose to the stable and put him in a stall. He looked around for a musket. There was not a spare one in sight.

He got back to Concord Green just as Amos Barrett and Dave Brown were forming up their companies. Little Abner Hosmer stood at the head of the column beating out a lilting tattoo on his drum. Tom Lincoln, no older than Ab, skirled a shrill marching tune on his fife. Then the two companies marched out in the direction of the Lexington road, the men's muskets shouldered in military fashion, their heads held high, their feet slapping the dirt of the road in an unsuccessful effort to keep step to the tempo of the music.

Rob ran to the head of the company and fell into step beside Captain Brown.

"Son," the captain said, "what're you doin' here? You ain't even got a musket."

The rattle of the drum and the skirling of the fife were making a wild sort of music in Rob's head as the column quick-marched down the road. He felt good, better than he had ever felt in his life. His feet were light as feathers, and the air that he sucked into his lungs was clean and bracing. The blood raced madly through his veins, and he could feel his heart pounding. Right now, he felt like he could whip any ten British soldiers in Gen'ral Gage's army!

"Well, sir," he said in reply to Captain Brown's question, "when we meet the Redcoats and the lead starts flyin', I figure there ought to be quite a few brand-new British-made muskets lying around. I aim to pick me out the best one I can find."

Captain Dave Brown threw his head back and laughed.

"That's the spirit, boy," he said. "And while you're at it, pick yourself out a full ca'tridge case."

The column swung down the road for nearly a mile. Then Rob saw a small, spindly-legged figure appear over the crest of the ridge and run down toward the marching Minute Men. The man had a bandage around his head and a musket hanging from his right hand.

"That's Mutt Cooper from Lexington," Rob shouted. " 'Pears like he was in the fight."

Dave Brown held his hand up over his head, and the marching column shuffled to a stop. The men in the rear ranks banged into those in front of them before the forward motion of the whole company could be arrested.

Mutt Cooper scrambled over a roadside wall and came up to Captain Brown. He looked quizzically at the captain, then ran his eye back over the column that numbered little more than a hundred men. He shook his red head.

"Hi don't know where ye think ye're goin'," he said, "but Hi can tell ye that th' whole blasted British army is less'n a quarter of a mile down th' road. Ye're marchin' square into 'em."

"That's what we aim to do," Dave Brown said. "We aim to stop 'em before they get to Concord Town."

Mutt brushed the stubble on his narrow chin with his fingers, and again he slowly shook his head.

"Man," he said gravely, " 'ave ye taken leave o' yer senses?" He pointed to Rob. "This lad 'ere can tell ye that there's near eight hundred sojers in yon column. Hi don't like King German George no better'n any of ye. An' far less than most, Hi'll be bound, for Hi've got me own good reasons. But like 'im or not as ye will, the British Redcoat

[*120*]

is th' finest sojer in th' world, bar none. An' that Major Pitcairn, wot's leadin' 'em, is the best one of th' lot."

This was a long speech for Mutt, and he paused to catch his breath.

"Not an hour ago, that column comin' along 'ere run over Cap'n John Parker's comp'ny in Lexington like they was slaughterin' pigs in a sty." He touched the blood-stained bandage on his head. "Hi was there, an' Hi know."

As he spoke, the first ranks of the British column appeared over a rise not five hundred yards away. The morning sun glinted off the metal front-plates of their tall, bearskin hats and the glittering points of their fixed bayonets. The column poured up over the rise, rank after rank, filling the narrow road from wall to wall as a flash flood fills and overflows the banks of a dry riverbed.

The mounted officer at their head reined up his black horse and held his hand over his head. The river of Redcoats came to a momentary stop.

"Look ye, Cap'n," Mutt Cooper pleaded. "Ye've got nary a chance. In th' open like this, that army'll mow yer men down like grain afore a scythe. Turn round. Git back to Concord. If we must fight 'em, let's do hit on our own terms, not theirs."

Captain David Brown made a quick decision. He raised his arm, and his voice:

"Ha-bout—*face!*"

The Minute Men looked bewildered.

"We'll fight 'em, men!" Dave Brown shouted. "But not here. The colonel said not to stand agin' 'em. So we won't. We'll fight 'em in our own way, Injun style!"

A ragged cheer went up from the Minute Men.

To Rob's amazement, it was answered by a cheer from the massed ranks of the Redcoats.

"Drummer boy! Fifer!" Captain Brown's voice bellowed. "Get yerselves to the head of the column and lead us back to town in style!"

Abner Hosmer and Tom Lincoln ran to the head of the now reversed line. Captain Brown followed. "All right, now," he ordered. "Play!"

Ab and Tom struck up a lively tune that rose into the still air of the little valley. It was a rollicking, rhythmic tune that New England people called "Yankee Doodle." It was good music to march by, and the men of the company whistled as they retraced their steps toward Concord.

Rob had stayed where he was, his eyes on the British column. Now he saw a group of soldiers skirt around the sides of the column and move to its head. Instead of the familiar red, their coats were yellow, orange, and blue. Each man carried a a drum or a fife.

When the British band had formed at the head of the column, Major Pitcairn gave a signal. The musicians struck up a marching tune of their own, and the Redcoat line swung into motion again.

Now the two armies were marching sedately down the road as though there was no threat of war on this side of the ocean—the Concord Minute companies in the lead, the Redcoats less than five hundred yards behind. The music of the Colonials' one drummer boy and fifer was overwhelmed by the volume of the British band.

Once the column got moving, Rob and Mutt Cooper made their way to the head of it. Dave Brown and Amos Barrett were swinging along in the lead, side by side.

"I'll say one thing for the bloody Redcoats," Amos Barrett grinned. "They're givin' us grand music!"

[*123*]

CHAPTER TEN

Concord Bridge

HALF a mile from town, the British music stopped. Looking over his shoulder, Rob saw the musicians step out of line and fade back into the rear ranks. Infantrymen took their places, and the British column came marching on. A fan of Light Infantrymen spread out to the low ridges on the moving column's left and right.

"Let's git!" Dave Brown shouted. "On the double!"

The Minute Men stepped up their pace to a trot. When they came once more into Concord Green, most of the men were gasping for breath.

Colonel Barrett sat his horse in front of the tavern.

"Over the bridge, Dave!" the colonel said curtly. "Go past Elisha Jones's house, and git on tother side of the river."

The company broke up as the men scrambled down the road and across the narrow bridge. Under Captain Brown's direction, they took up positions on the high ground of the slope, behind boulders and stone walls. Rob went with them, and now he looked over the rim of a low wall down at the village Green below. He still didn't have a musket. There had been no glorious battle in which he could pick up a new British one.

Now that the American defenders had evacuated Concord, the Redcoat column came pouring in. Soldiers swarmed over the Green in a scarlet-coated wave. There was a disorganized milling about as the Redcoats broke ranks. Then a fat officer rode out, mounted on a milk-white horse.

"That's Colonel Smith," Mutt Cooper whispered. The little cockney had stayed close to Rob's side. "Let's see what the fat little rooster— Glory be! He's gonna pass 'em in review!"

Major Pitcairn rode out and took his place beside Colonel Smith, his black horse standing out in sharp contrast to the colonel's milk-white.

The air above the Green was filled with crisp commands, and the British quickly formed their ranks again. Then, company by company, the army wheeled into line and paraded past their commanding officers. The band played, the marching feet stepped high in perfect precision, the polished bayonets on the shouldered muskets glittered in the sun. All over the side of the hill west of the little bridge that spanned the Concord River, Minute Men abandoned caution and stood bolt upright. Their mouths hung open in wonderment as they watched the colorful show.

When the last company had filed past the reviewing officers, the Redcoats fell out of formation and scattered over the village.

One group of a dozen soldiers entered the town house on the Green and emerged a few minutes later, yelling and whooping, dragging a score of wooden gun carriages behind them. They piled the carriages into a heap in the street and set fire to them. Light blue spirals of woodsmoke curled upward from them into the sky. Other squads burned houses, broke into storerooms around the Green and came out lugging barrels of flour and sacks of provisions. The men smashed in the sides of the barrels with their musket butts. Then they rolled them into the millpond behind the tavern. While all this activity was going on, Rob could see the British officers lounging in front of the tavern or passing in and out from the taproom.

Then Mutt Cooper yanked at Rob's sleeve and pointed to the other side of the Green. Four or five companies of Redcoats, over a hundred in all, Rob figured, detached themselves from the hustling mob of soldiers and formed into ranks. Stepping smartly, their officers led them out of town and down the winding road to the bridge that crossed the Concord River. This was directly beneath the position that Colonel Barrett's men occupied on the top of the ridge. When they came to the bridge, the British column split up. Half of the troops took positions on the town side of the river. The rest marched across the bridge and began to spread out over the lower part of the opposite slope.

On the ridge above him, Rob heard a loud voice:

"Let's go git 'em, Colonel!"

There were answering yells. And then the whole army of nearly a thousand Minute Men topped the rise and swarmed down over the steep hillside. They were marching in a column of two's, with Captain Isaac Davis, of the Acton Company, in the lead. Strutting beside the captain was little Abner Hosmer, bravely beating out a lively march-step on his drum. Behind these two, the Minute Men came on relentlessly, their faces grim, their muskets cocked and held at the ready in front of them. As the column progressed down the hill, the scattered groups of men who had taken up positions behind walls and boulders joined in the march. Rob and Mutt Cooper fell into line with the rest.

"Ye'd best git back, boy," Mutt said. "Havin'

no firearm, there's little good ye can do."

But Rob was caught up in the grand excitement of the moment. His head was ringing, and he could feel his heart thumping under his shirt like a wooden maul pounding at a fence post. Men were crowded close to him, before and behind, and he was swept along on the marching wave.

Below him, not too far away now, he saw the British officer at the bridge shout a command. The Redcoats on the near side of the river hurried back to join their comrades. The British formed into solid ranks at the Concord end of the bridge, their muskets held to their shoulders in firing position, and waited.

The Rebel army marched on like an avenging host—"embattled farmers" from Acton, Chelmsford, and Weston—wheelwrights, wainwrights, carpenters, blacksmiths—storekeepers, clerks, school teachers, preachers—men who had kissed their children good-by in the early hours of the morning and gone out of their houses, muskets in hand—men who valued Liberty more than life. Straight on they marched, into the muzzles of the British muskets.

It seemed like suicide, Rob thought, walking like this into the massed guns of troops that Mutt Cooper had said were the finest soldiers in the world. But Captain Davis and little Abner Hosmer and all the men behind them strode long-legged down the hill, never missing a step.

Suddenly, without warning, there was a deafening blast of fire from the British ranks, and a cloud of black smoke blanketed the bridge. Rob saw Captain Davis pitch forward on his face. At the same instant, little Abner Hosmer threw his drumsticks convulsively into the air and collapsed. His pudgy body rolled over twice, like a stone going downhill, and then came to a stop and lay still. A man on Rob's right threw his musket to his shoulder, but a bullet from the Redcoats' second volley struck him before he could pull the trigger. For a split second he stood bolt upright, as though wondering what had hit him. Then his legs folded underneath him, and he slumped down into the grass.

Almost as if the volley from the British had been a signal, the Rebel column spread out on either side of itself like a giant fan. The men raced forward, in a broad, thin line now, firing as they ran. Rob saw a Redcoat on the bridge reel, drop his musket, and tumble with a splash into the river. Two others beside him went down almost at the same time. The air was filled with the booming and cracking of musket fire and the whine of flying balls. Wisps of stinging black powder smoke rolled up the hill like miniature storm clouds.

Rob found himself running forward with the rest. On all sides of him, men were yelling at the top of their voices, stopping to aim and fire, kneeling to reload their muskets, then running on. There seemed to be no order to the furious downhill charge. Nothing but a bedlam of noise and confusion, like bad dreams Rob could remember, in which he kept running on and on without knowing why.

Suddenly his feet flew out from under him. He

stumbled forward and fell heavily. Instinctively, he threw his arms out wide to break the fall.

"I've been hit!" The thought raced through Rob's mind like a lightning flash, and for a moment he lay still, his eyes closed, a sick feeling of awful fear flooding his whole body.

Then he realized that his outstretched hands were touching something cold and hard. He opened his eyes. It was the barrel of a musket lying in the grass. Next to it were the sprawling legs of a man. With a shudder, Rob realized that he had tripped over the body of a fallen Minute Man. He scrambled to his feet, the musket grasped in his hand.

The Minute Man lay spread-eagled. Next to one outstretched hand was a powder horn and a buckskin shot bag that had slipped off the man's shoulder when he fell. A wave of horror swept over Rob at the thought of taking a dead man's possessions. But he made himself reach down and pick them up. The dead man couldn't use them now, but he, Rob Gordon, could. Guns and powder were too scarce in Massachusetts Colony to let any go to waste. He slung the horn and bag over his shoulder and started on.

Now the charge had left Rob behind. The first wave of attacking Americans had reached the river and were splashing through it, keeping up a steady barrage of fire as they went. Another Redcoat went down, and another, to add to the pile of lifeless British soldiers that lay sprawled in grotesque positions on the bridge.

Then the unexpected happened. Before Rob's amazed eyes, the British infantry, who a moment before had been formed up in solid ranks, broke and ran in panic. The Redcoats in the front ranks turned on the files behind them, shoving, pushing, tripping over each other in their frantic efforts to escape. Some threw down their guns. An officer who tried to stop them was knocked backwards into the water.

At the sight of the panicked British, a fresh chorus of yelling went up from the onrushing Rebel line. Men scrambled through the water, waving their guns above their heads. A few, in the excitement, fired wildly into the air. Some of the Minute Men raced across the planks of the now deserted bridge, leaping over the bodies of the fallen Redcoats as they ran. By the time Rob reached the riverbank, a good part of the Yankee

[*133*]

force had crossed to the other side. He splashed through the water and joined them.

The last of the running Redcoats were rounding a sharp bend in the road a hundred yards ahead, in their desperate flight to the safety of Concord Green and the main force of the British army. A handful of Rebels kept after them, but for the most part the Minute Men had stopped. The overpowering momentum of their charge apparently had been halted by their easy victory and the sight of the panicked and retreating British Regulars.

Rob made out the bandy-legged figure of Mutt Cooper running down the road toward the bend. He paused only for a second, then followed after him.

He caught up with the little cockney on a slope just around the turn of the road. Here the pursuing Minute Men had stopped and were taking stock of the situation. No one seemed to be in command, and the men looked from one to the other as they tried to decide what to do.

"If ye'll take my advice," Mutt was saying, "ye'll wait till Colonel Barrett gets 'ere. No use takin' on th' whole British army out in th' open."

"I'll go fetch the colonel," a man volunteered. He started back up the road to the bridge.

Then Mutt spotted Rob, and his lean face blossomed into a big grin.

"Well now, lad," he beamed. "That was a right smart fight." He shook his red head in pleased puzzlement. "Never thought Hi'd live to see th' day when British Regulars tucked in their tails an' ran at the first sound o' gunfire." He clapped Rob on the shoulder. "Hi see ye found yerself a weapon."

He took the musket from Rob's hand and examined it expertly.

"Old an' rusty. Might hexplode the first time ye squeezed hit off. Leave hit 'ere, and let's go see if we can find ye a proper gun. Ought to be a sight o' British Brown Bess muskets litterin' th' riverbank back yonder."

Rob was glad to get rid of the gun he had taken from the dead Minute Man. He propped it reverently against a tree and looped the old powder horn and the bullet bag over its muzzle.

Then he and Mutt retraced their steps back down the road to Concord bridge.

CHAPTER ELEVEN

The Bloody Road

IT WAS high noon. The sun, standing straight overhead, felt good on Rob's back and shoulders as he sat on the slope of a hill overlooking Concord Town. He balanced a brand-new British Brown Bess musket upright between his knees. Over his shoulder hung a shiny leather cartridge case. Both pieces of equipment bore an imprint that identified them as the property of His Majesty, King George the Third.

Well, Your Majesty, Rob thought as he tightened the flint in the lock of the Brown Bess, they belong to Minute Man Rob Gordon now!

In the leather case were about three dozen cartridges, neat rolls of paper that contained both

[136]

powder and ball. Rob had never used this kind of modern firing charge before, but he knew how it was done. You held the cartridge by the bullet end and bit off the paper at the other. You shook enough powder for priming into the pan. Then you poured the rest of the powder down the barrel, dropped in the ball, and rammed the paper firmly on top of it as wadding. A big improvement, he thought, over his old-fashioned powder horn and bullet bag that hung above the mantelpiece in John Buckman's tavern.

It had been two hours since the fight at the bridge. The Minute Men who had made the charge were now scattered over the slopes on both sides of the valley. Some were sitting down, resting, as Rob was doing now. Others moved around aimlessly in small groups, talking in quiet tones as though awed by the fact that an armed clash with British Regulars had come at last. But every man kept a restless eye cocked on the British troops that still occupied the town.

The Rebel force was now about twice the size it had been when the Redcoats fired the volley that opened the battle. Companies had been drifting in all morning from the more distant towns around, too late for the brief, fierce fight at the bridge, but ready and waiting for whatever was to come next.

At the moment, however, no one knew what that might be. The commanding officers of the Minute Men, Colonel Barrett and Major Buttrick, had disappeared, and nobody seemed to have any idea where they had gone. So, in the absence of leaders to tell them what to do, the men stood around and waited for something to happen, as common soldiers have done since the beginnings of warfare.

Now there was a new burst of activity among the British on the Green below. The soldiers had commandeered half a dozen wagons and carriages, and into these they were loading their comrades who had been wounded at the bridge fight. At last, it appeared, the Redcoat column was getting ready to move out and return to Boston.

Well, they had precious little to show for all their trouble, Rob thought, except a few dead and wounded on both sides and a hundred barrels of flour dumped into the millpond. He wondered if Private Howe would get his commission, now that the expedition he had told the general would be easy had turned out so disastrously.

Rob watched the preparations idly. Then suddenly he jumped to his feet with a loud shout of protest.

Mutt Cooper had been lying stretched out at Rob's side, staring up into the sky and munching on a blade of grass.

"Wot's up, lad?" he asked.

"My horse!" Rob yelled, pointing. "They're stealing my horse!"

Down on the Green, a Regular was leading Roman Nose across the grass. Even at that distance, there was no mistaking the big bay. The soldier prepared to hitch him to one of the wagons. The horse's ears were laid back, and he was stomping a forefoot as though he resented being handled by a stranger. But the Redcoat must have been used to horses, for he stroked Roman Nose's muzzle and patted his neck, and in a moment the animal quieted down and backed obediently into the shafts.

"They're just swappin' 'im for that Brown Bess," Mutt grinned.

Rob's face was red with sudden anger. He shook his fist at the distant red-coated figure.

"They can't do that!" the boy cried. "He's private property!"

"Looks like they're doin' hit all the same," Mutt grunted.

"That's just plain horse stealing!" Rob's out-thrust jaw clipped off the words. "I'll get him back—if I have to follow the thievin' Lobster-backs all the way into Boston and steal him over again."

The cockney's grin softened when he saw how deeply Rob felt about the horse.

"Sure—ye'll get 'im back. But if hit 'appens ye don't, remember this is war now, lad. An' a man's got to make a lot o' sacrifices, as ye might say, in wartime."

Now the British had once more formed up into an orderly column of companies and regiments, and were beginning to march out of town, the wagons and carriages sandwiched in the middle of the slowly moving line. Squads of Light In-fantry flanked out smartly on either side of the point. The Redcoats behaved as coolly as if they were going through a maneuver on a drill field. It seemed hard to believe these were the same veteran troops who had panicked and run like scared rabbits this morning at the bridge!

As the British column flowed off the Green and

into the Lexington Road, the watchers on the ridges moved with them. There had been no command, because no high-ranking officer was present to give it. The Americans moved as if by a common impulse, spreading over the slopes of the low hills and down onto the flats. No one fired, and there was very little talking as the Minute Men moved silently along on either side of the marching British. It seemed almost as though the Yankees were escorting the Redcoat army out of town.

Then one of the Grenadiers bringing up the rear of the British column did a strangely unmilitary thing. British infantrymen were not taught to fire individually, nor even to aim their weapons. Instead, they were trained to fight from a solid front, leveling their muskets to shoulder height and firing them blindly in a volley on command.

But this man, apparently shaken by the long night's march, the panic at the bridge, and now the sight of two thousand Rebel soldiers silently following the army's orderly retreat, turned suddenly and fired his musket at the horde of Minute Men.

Regulars began dropping on every side

Like a match applied to the fuse of a bomb, his
shot touched off a fury of firing. Individually and
in groups of two, four, six, or a dozen, the Massachusetts men swarmed over the fields in the
rear and on either side of the Redcoat column.
They took refuge behind stone walls, trees, rocks,
and piles of fence rails, and began pouring a
withering fire into the closely packed British ranks.

The column, which a moment before had been
moving along in a precise and orderly manner,
now shuddered to a standstill as Regulars began
dropping on every side. Rob could hear officers
shouting frantic commands over the crashing din
of the gunfire in their attempts to close up the
shattered ranks. Some of the soldiers dropped their
muskets and tried to help the wounded into the
wagons. Others leaped to the heads of the terror-
stricken horses that were rearing and bucking and
trying to kick themselves free of their harness.
The sides of the road were littered with sprawling,
red-coated soldiers.

Rob, with Mutt Cooper at his side, raced down
the hill for the shelter of a stone wall about forty
yards from the road. When he reached it, he
threw himself face down on the ground. He lay
still for a moment to catch his breath and give his

[*143*]

heart a chance to quiet down. Then he peeked up cautiously over the edge—and his eyes stared straight into the leveled muskets of a squad of Redcoats that had stepped out of the column and now stood facing the wall in a solid front.

He ducked a split second before the British volley boomed. The shrill whistle of a dozen musket balls whined over his head, and a cloud of black smoke darkened the sky. A few yards on his left, a farmer who had chosen that moment to raise his gun over the piled-up stones, was knocked backward as though he had been struck by a cannon ball. He fell like a stone.

Rob could hear the drumming of his heart over the furious bang and rattle of the firing. His hands were shaking so violently that it was only by gripping the barrel and stock with all his strength that he could hold his musket.

He steeled himself and looked over the wall again. The British squad had melted back into the ragged column. Rob aimed his musket into the milling mass of red uniforms and blindly jerked the trigger. Without waiting to see the effect of his shot, he fell back into the protecting shelter of the wall.

[*144*]

"Keep yer 'ead down, bucky boy!"

It was Mutt Cooper, stretched out beside Rob and supporting himself on one elbow as he rammed a fresh load into his musket's muzzle. His teeth flashed white through lips that were blackened all around by powder stains from biting the cartridge ends.

"Don't h'expose yerself, lad. Peek through th' chinks betwixt th' stones, an' pick yerself a target 'fore ye raise up. Like this."

The cockney squinted between the narrow cracks in the wall. Then, apparently having selected a target to his liking, he raised his musket over the wall, took aim, fired, and dropped back to the ground in one swift motion.

"All Yankees think as 'ow they're safe long as they're pertected from th' neck down." He grinned. "But don't you be makin' that mistake, boy, for ye'll make it only once."

As he talked, he bit the end from another cartridge and began loading his piece again.

He nodded his head and winked.

"That 'un made number four."

Rob realized that he had been crouching, doing nothing, his hands still shaking and his heart still pounding. Now he took a cartridge from the leather case hanging over his shoulder and began to reload the Brown Bess. It was awkward work, trying to ram the load securely into the musket barrel while lying almost prone. And before the job was done, Mutt Cooper had fired twice more. By the time Rob hunched his face up close to the wall to look for another target from between the chinks in the stones, the end of the column had passed out of range. Mutt was standing erect, and now Rob did so too. He looked curiously around.

A dozen British dead lay in the road. To Rob's right, a brown-coated Minute Man was sprawled over the wall, both arms outstretched. A few yards away on his other side was the body of the man who had been hit by the British volley that had so narrowly missed Rob's head.

"Wait 'ere, lad."

Mutt leaped over the wall and ran to the road. In a few moments he returned, carrying three cartridge cases. He slung two of them over his shoulder and handed the third to Rob.

"Don't be squeamish, boy. Take this. Them poor beggers yonder won't need 'em any more. Come on!"

When the firing had started, Rob and Mutt had
been on the slope at the British rear. The position
they had taken behind the wall was close to the
end of the straggling column. Now the last of
the Redcoats was forty or fifty yards farther on up
the road, thus making the total range about twice
that distance. A smooth-bore musket like Rob's
Brown Bess wasn't accurate at much more than
fifty yards. He sure wished he had one of those
Pennsylvania long rifles, like the ones he'd heard
men talk about around John Buckman's fire at
night. They claimed a good rifleman could knock a
squirrel out of a tree at two hundred yards. Rob
had never seen one of these fabulous guns, but he
wished he had one now!

Mutt trotted off in the wake of the British column, quartering up the slope, and Rob jogged
along at his side.

"We'll go round 'em and get close to th' 'ead
o' th' column," the cockney said, speaking over
his shoulder as he ran. "That way we'll get ourselves a crack at th' 'ole bloody h'army."

On both sides of the road, Rob saw other figures
in brown coats scurrying along the slopes or
through the flat fields to get into position abreast
of the moving British. Down below, on the road

that wound like a twisting river between the hills, the battered column of Redcoats pressed doggedly on.

They passed the middle of the column where the wagons and carriages lumbered along. The drivers whipped the horses and tugged at the lines to keep the bewildered beasts under control in the midst of the furious noise and near-panic that was going on all around them.

Suddenly one of the horses screamed, reared, and fell heavily sideways. The carriage to which it was hitched careened on its two left wheels, teetered for half a second, and toppled over. The wounded British soldiers inside spilled out like potatoes from a sack. The thrashing horse and wrecked carriage blocked the narrow road, and the struggling infantrymen following along behind separated and flowed around it like water dividing to pass a stone in a riverbed.

Rob thought of Roman Nose. He looked down at the column as he ran and tried to spot the bay. But at that distance, with the air over the road obscured by a heavy fog of powder smoke, it was impossible to tell one horse from another.

" 'Ere we go!" Mutt Cooper swung his arm in a

forward motion and cut sharply down the hillside. At another angle in a stone wall, again about thirty or forty yards from the Redcoats, he dropped to the ground. Rob did the same.

"Now," the little cockney said grimly, " 'ere's a good place to give 'em wot for."

They were slightly behind the head of the British column now. The first panic created by the sudden assault of the Minute Men had passed, and although the marching Redcoat regiments were still a stumbling shambles, the officers had managed to bring a semblance of order out of the confusion. From time to time, British squads wheeled out of the moving line, faced the walls with leveled muskets, and fired a volley. Then, as they faded back into the column, Rob could see them methodically reloading their pieces at their officers' shouted commands.

The British line of march was leaving the road behind it liberally sprinkled with the scarlet coats of the dead and wounded. But the green grass and the freshly plowed earth of the fields behind the stone walls was also dotted with the still forms of brown-coated Americans.

Rob had never seen a man killed before, and

[*149*]

the sight made his stomach churn and soaked his shirt with clammy sweat. Many a time he had taken aim over the barrel of his old musket at the shoulder of a deer in the woods. He had seen the animal leap forward and somersault over its antlers as the buckshot tore into its heart. But that was different. Anyway, that was meat for John Buckman's table—just as the hogs they slaughtered each fall turned into hams and sausages. But to sight down the barrel at the figure of a man, and then see him stagger backward, twist around grotesquely and fall . . .

Suddenly Rob wanted to be sick. He buried his face in his hands and tried to get control of himself.

He felt a hand on his shoulder.

"Easy, lad, Hi know 'ow ye feel. This is dirty work, an' Hi don't like hit a mite better'n you do. But they started it, lad, not us. A man's got to fight sometimes fer wot he believes in. And when fightin' starts, a few people is bound to get theirselves 'urt. So just you try not to—"

While Mutt was still speaking, his hand slammed violently down on the back of Rob's neck and pushed his face into the dirt. At the same instant, the blast of another volley tore over their heads. Before the echo of the sound faded, Mutt raised himself up and discharged his musket at the British line. His shot was immediately followed by three others, from Rob's gun and those of two Minute Men who shared the shelter of their corner of the wall.

Suddenly a huge Redcoat, his face under the shaggy bearskin hat twisted with rage and hatred, burst out of the ranks and charged crazily at the wall with his bayonet leveled.

Rob looked around wildly. Mutt and the two other Minute Men were frantically reloading. Rob realized that he could never load his own gun in time. The charging Britisher was now less than twenty feet away, his long legs covering the plowed ground in giant strides.

For a moment it seemed as though time had come to a standstill, frozen into this single, heart-stopping second. The Grenadier was certain to bayonet at least one of the four Yankees before he could be stopped!

Then from the British squad that had fired the volley, two other Redcoats burst out after the first, yelling as they came.

The appearance of the second and third Grenadier snapped Rob out of his momentary spell of
buck fever. He sprang to his feet and vaulted over
the wall in one leap. Holding his musket in both
hands like a club, he slammed it with all his

strength across the gleaming bayonet which now loomed a scant two feet away. The force of the blow brought the charging soldier to an abrupt stop and jolted the musket out of his hands. He threw his arms out wide, and his musket spun away from his outstretched fingertips. He tripped over his own feet and fell heavily forward.

The sight of their comrade going down halted the furious charge of the other two Redcoats. They stopped, wheeled around in their tracks and ran back for the comparative safety of the massed column. Before they had taken more than two steps, Mutt's musket spoke. It was echoed by the gun blasts of the two men who stood next to him. The three Grenadiers lay still.

"Nice work, lad!" Mutt said. "Ye saved our skins that time fer sure."

Then he turned his attention back to the grim business of the day.

Twice more Rob and Mutt changed their positions, moving to new vantage points as the badly mauled British column staggered down the bloody road between blistering walls of musketry. Now the two of them were behind a rock pile on the slope above Lexington, and the Redcoat army was entering the town. As if by common consent, the Minute Men had slackened their fire as the British marched past the houses, fearful that stray bullets might hit children or townspeople. But aside from the moving British, there was no sign of life on the Green or in the streets.

Rob had fired until the barrel of the Brown Bess was too hot to touch, and he was grateful for the respite. Since stopping the charging Grenadier, he knew that he was just as much of a soldier as any of the other men behind the stone walls. He knew that dozens of other boys, his age and younger, were fighting shoulder to shoulder beside their fathers and brothers today. He knew that the British had to be beaten at all costs.

But, just the same, he had been aiming low, for the marching, mud-stained legs. A wounded man, he argued to himself, would contribute as much to a British defeat as a dead one. Maybe even more, since the wounded were an extra burden for the rest.

It was amazing, Rob thought, as he looked down at the battered army, how the British officers had been able to keep the column moving along through the pitiless storm of gunfire that poured in on them from all sides. He had to admire the Redcoats' courage. A few had broken and run at the first shots. Yet for the most part, at least up to now, they had managed to stage an orderly retreat.

But the running fight had been going on for more than two frightful hours, and now it seemed that the British had come at last to the end of their endurance. There was very little firing from the column. Likely, Rob reckoned, they were running shy of powder and ball. He saw some of the men throw away their guns and equipment and bolt for the safety of the surrounding wooded hills. Some simply dropped out of line and sank wearily down by the side of the road.

Rob wondered if the officers might line the army up on the Green and surrender. He didn't see how human beings could stand much more of such terrible punishment.

Then, without warning, the whole picture down below changed. A great cheer went up from the weary Redcoats. The column came to life again, and the men moved forward at a brisk trot.

Mutt Cooper, who had been taking advantage of the slight slackening of fire to stretch his tired bones out on the ground, snapped to alarmed attention.

"Somethin's up, lad!" he yelled and ran for the brow of the hill that cut off the view of the country beyond Lexington. Rob grabbed his musket and followed.

As they trotted over the top of the rise, Rob saw a sight that stopped him with the shocking, sickening force of a blow in the pit of the stomach.

A second British army, larger even than this one retreating down the road, had come out from Boston. Now they were forming a line of battle on the shoulder of a hill that commanded a long slope leading down into Lexington. Artillerymen were busily dragging two cannon into firing position.

As Rob's shocked eyes took in the scene, one of the cannon belched out a cloud of heavy black smoke, followed seconds later by a thunderous explosion that sounded like the slamming of a giant door. Then the second cannon boomed.

Now all the crackle and banging of musketry had stopped as the bewildered Minute Men on the hillsides tried to adjust themselves to this sudden and unexpected change in the pattern of the fight.

"We're in fer hit, now, lad," Mutt Copper said, his voice low. "We've got a proper battle on our 'ands."

In the road below, the British column was running pell mell through the town in the direction of the reinforcements. They yelled, shouted, waved their guns over their heads. Rob watched, then he was jerked abruptly back to the reality of the moment by Mutt's cry:

" 'Ware! Be'ind ye! Flankers!"

Rob wheeled just in time to see a party of six Redcoat Light Infantrymen come around the side of the hill on his right.

He threw his musket to his shoulder. But before he could aim or squeeze the trigger, the inside of his head burst into a flaming, spinning ball. He could feel himself fall, slowly, floatingly, as though he was sinking down through deep, dark waters.

He didn't know it when he hit the ground.

CHAPTER TWELVE

Old Roman Nose

ROB groaned and opened his eyes. Then he clamped them tight shut again as a ray of light burned into his brain like the stab of a red-hot knife. He lay still for a moment to let a wave of sudden sickness wash over his body, and when it had subsided he tried again.

This time it didn't hurt so much. He rolled his eyeballs cautiously in their sockets in an attempt to look around.

He was lying stretched out, he could tell, on a broad puncheon table in the public room of John Buckman's tavern, a blanket covering him and a pillow under his head. Vaguely he heard a buzz of voices. A hazy face seemed to float above him.

Then the face swam into focus. It was Sary Williams.

Sary was gently wiping his cheeks with a cool, damp cloth when she saw him open his eyes.

"Rob!" Quickly she turned her head and called over her shoulder. "He's awake, Ma! Rob's awake!"

Rob touched his hand to his temple. His fingers felt a heavy bandage that was bound around his head like a heathen's turban. His skull, under the cloth, felt as though it had been kicked by a balky horse.

Then he heard John Buckman's booming voice.

"Welcome back to the land of the livin', lad. You gave us quite a turn there, when Mutt Cooper came draggin' ye in." He held a pewter mug to Rob's lips. "Here. Drink this down."

Sary helped him lift his head, and Rob gulped down a big swallow. The fiery liquid burned his throat and the inside of his stomach, but the shock of it started to sweep the cobwebs out of his brain.

"Wha—what happened?"

"You 'ad a near 'un, bucky boy!"

It was Mutt Cooper. The little Englishman sat

in a chair with one shoulder swathed in white bandages and his right arm in a sling. His face had been recently washed, but traces of black powder stain still remained around his lips. His teeth flashed in a good-natured grin.

"When them flankers flushed us, they got me in this shoulder same time as they got you. When I'd got back me wits, they'd moved on. Then Joel Perkins 'appened along, an' betwixt th' two of us we dragged and carried ye 'ere."

"You're a lucky lad, Rob," John Buckman said. "That musket ball just grazed the side o' yer forehead. Didn't much more than break the skin, but it raised a knot as big as a turkey egg."

Rob gingerly explored his bandaged head with the tips of his fingers. The first crashing pain had passed, and the dull ache was fading. Then his head suddenly cleared, and the whole scene on the slope above the town came back to him vividly. The British reinforcements spread out in battle line across the side of the hill! The battery of booming cannon! The flanking party that had surprised and shot him! And now, faintly through the open tavern door, he again heard the sound of popping muskets. They seemed to come from a long distance away.

[*160*]

Rob sat bolt upright and swung his legs over the table's edge. He hung on to the wide hand-hewn boards for a moment until his head, set swimming again by the sudden movement, once more had cleared.

"Mutt! The fight! The Redcoats brought up cannon! You saw them!"

"Go easy, lad," Mutt said. "Th' fight's still goin' 'ammer an' tongs. But th' battle's all over fer you and me. You did yer bit. Sit down an' rest."

Sary took his arm and helped him to a chair. He slumped into it gratefully.

"Now you just calm down a minute, Mr. Rob Gordon! You can't fight this old war all by your-self!" Sary scolded.

"The lass is right, Rob," John Buckman said. "You've had enough for one day."

"But Uncle John! The Redcoats have brought a whole new army out of Boston. Mutt and I saw them lined up on the hill beyond the Green. There must be thousands of them. They'll come back—"

"They won't come back. Not soon, Rob. Lord Percy—it is him, they say, that brought the main army out—thought to make a stand. But when he'd set up those cannon of his and looked around for somebody to shoot at, our boys had faded back behind the rocks and walls and started pepperin' the Redcoats with musket balls again."

"Us Yankees," Mutt Cooper grinned, "we learned a lesson today about 'ow to fight British Regulars."

John Buckman grinned back at him. "Some of us oldtimers learned that trick fightin' the Injuns back in the old French war."

Mrs. Williams bustled into the room carrying a steaming bowl.

"You drink this nice hot broth, Rob," she said. "It will put some strength back into those tired bones of yours."

The good smell of the broth made Rob realize that he was famished. He hadn't had anything to eat since supper the night before. He attacked the bowl greedily. With every spoonful he could feel strength and energy flowing into him, and in no time at all the bowl was empty.

Except for a slight soreness, the pain in his head had vanished completely. He was surprised to find that he didn't feel any worse for his encounter with the British musket ball.

Sary was flurrying about, taking away the empty bowl, bringing him a cup of tea, spreading the blanket over his knees. Then she adjusted the voluminous bandage that was still wrapped around his head.

"You say I wasn't cut much, Sary?"

"Why, no. Scarcely at all."

"Then can't we take this—this flour sack off my head?"

Sary smiled, untied the bandage, and gently unwrapped it. She touched the egg-sized lump lightly with her fingers.

"O-oh! What a bump! Does it hurt, Rob?"

Rob laughed. "Only when you fool with it."

She jerked her hand away.

"Don't worry, Sary. I was only funnin'. It doesn't hurt a bit. It even feels so good I think I'll take a little walk to stretch my legs."

Sary looked at him with a searching, sideways glance.

"Now see here, Rob! You're not going to try any fool tricks, are you?"

"Not me," Rob grinned. "You heard Mutt Cooper. The fightin's all over for me today. I'm just going out to get a breath of fresh air that isn't all fouled up with powder smoke."

He patted her gratefully on the arm, got up from his chair, and went quietly out through the kitchen. Over his shoulder he could see Mutt Cooper and John Buckman sitting at one of the tables, talking, and drinking hot buttered rum.

Outside, Rob looked up at the sky. It was about four o'clock, he reckoned. The air was cool and sweet, but a faint, acrid smell of powder fumes still mingled itself with the perfume of the dogwoods in the tavern's back yard. Far away, off in the direction of the Boston road, he could hear the distant crackle of musket fire. A dark cloud of smoke hung low over the hills.

He started walking rapidly in its direction.

The battle sounds grew louder and more familiar as he drew closer. In his mind, now, Rob was a veteran. He could picture the Minute Men fighting from behind their walls and trees. Aiming, firing, reloading, then moving to new positions farther forward along the British line—harassing the exhausted and battle-weary Redcoats every step of their long way back to Boston.

He stayed away from the road and kept to the ridges.

Once he met a party of powder-blackened Yankees tiredly trudging back toward Lexington. One of them was Joel Perkins, the man John Buckman said had helped Mutt Cooper bring him in.

"Hi there, boy!" Perkins grinned through the dirt and grime on his face. "I figured that skullin' you got would keep you down a spell."

"How's the fight going, Mr. Perkins?"

"It's just about all over but the last hoo-raw. Wouldn't you say, boys?"

The men with him nodded their agreement.

"We run outa powder an' shot, so we figured to call it a day's work. We ain't had any sleep since yesterday, an' we're just about clean whipped. Reckon, though, there's still enough of the boys that come up this mornin' to see that Lord Percy's Redcoats get kept company."

Rob started to move on past them.

"You keep yer eye peeled, son," Joel Perkins warned. "When I say it's just about all over, I don't mean that dang near as many musket balls ain't still a-flyin' as have been all day long. You got in th' way of one of 'em today. No call to invite another'n."

"Thank you, Mr. Perkins. I'll be careful," Rob said and continued on his way.

Remembering the party of flankers that had surprised him earlier, Rob was cautious as he made his way over the rolling hills in the direction of the battle noises. Then he rounded a small stand of fir trees, and the running fight was once more spread out before him. He was on high ground now, well out of musket range. But aside from the fact that now he was in no danger, the pattern was the same as it had been all down the road from Concord.

There were more British in the column now and, it seemed to Rob, fewer Americans firing at them. But still the road in the Redcoats' wake was dotted with the scarlet uniforms of fallen men, and the shrill shouts of the officers floated up over the crash and din of the gunfire as they tried to hurry the floundering column along.

As Rob watched, the blood began pounding again in his temples, and the excitement of the fight below sent a cold tingle racing along his spine. He had just about made up his mind to slip down to the road, pick up a musket and cartridge case, and get back into the battle, when he saw a movement in the trees behind him and to his right. He dropped flat on his stomach and twisted his head around slowly.

His eyes caught the flash of a green skirt and the gleam of yellow hair.

"Sary!"

Rob jumped to his feet and ran to the girl. She stepped out from the shelter of the trees to meet him. Her face was pale, but her eyes sparkled and she stamped her little foot on the ground.

"You come away from there, Rob Gordon! Don't you dare go down over this hill!"

Rob grasped her shoulders with both hands and shook her hard.

"Sary! You looney little fool!" He pulled her back toward the shelter of the little patch of woods. "What in the name of sense are you doing here? Come on! I'm taking you straight back to your ma!"

Sary shook herself free. She ran to the brow of the hill and stood still for a moment, gazing fascinated at the mad confusion in the Boston road.

Rob stepped up to her and put a protective arm around her shoulders. Silently, the boy and the girl stood on the hill and stared down at the madness going on beneath them. Then Rob gently pulled her away.

"Come on, Sary. We're going home."

Sary was about to turn, when suddenly she shrieked and pointed.

"Rob! Look yonder! They've got Roman Nose!"

Rob stared in the direction of her pointing

finger. There was a confused shambles on the road directly below. Then Rob saw Roman Nose. The wagon he was pulling—the same one Rob had seen the Redcoat hitch him to this morning—had been forced into a ditch at the side of the road. One wheel was broken off, and the wagon sagged down on its axle. The driver had leaped from his seat and was now alternately tugging at the bay's bridle and then stepping back and lashing him unmercifully with a heavy whip.

Roman Nose was trapped. Securely hitched between the shafts of the crippled wagon, he was unable to move. Rob heard him whinny shrilly—a high-pitched scream of terror—and then lash out furiously with his hind hoofs. His iron shoes caught the singletree behind him and shattered it. Under the force of the blow, the wagon, already unbalanced by its broken wheel, crashed over on its side.

The near shaft splintered and broke, but the big gelding was still attached to the wagon by the tracechains and the shaft on his off side. The weight of the wagon pulled him over. He staggered and went to his knees. The driver, now in near panic, brought the whip down cruelly across

The driver brought the whip down cruelly across the fallen horse's back

the fallen horse's back and shoulders. Roman Nose screamed again. Then the wind whipped a cloud of black powder smoke over the road and almost obscured the scene.

Rob took one look at what was going on below him. Then he was off and running.

"Sary!" he yelled back over his shoulder. "Go home, Sary! Go back home!"

His hand reached around for the short hunting knife that he always carried at his belt. It was there. He ran on.

Now he was close to the second wall from the road. Musket balls were whining and screeching all around him. He hurdled the wall, running between two surprised Minute Men who had taken shelter there, and raced for the low wall that edged the road itself.

"Hey, you! Come back here!"

He heard the shout from the startled Colonials as he dived to the ground behind the wall and paused for a moment to catch his breath. On the ground at his feet was a stout length of wood, two feet long and as big around as a man's wrist. He picked it up and peered over the stones.

He was only twenty feet away from the wrecked

wagon. He saw Roman Nose trying to struggle to his feet as the British driver lashed him with the whip. Then he jumped over the wall.

He crashed into the middle of the moving British column. A Grenadier, running along the side of the road, banged into him and knocked him back against the wall. He recovered his footing and plunged on into the struggling mob of soldiers. In the noise of the crashing musket fire and the confused milling of the men, no one seemed to notice that he was not wearing a red coat. He fought his way through, against the current of shouting, sweating, elbowing, frantic infantrymen.

When he came to the broken wagon, the driver was raising his whip to bring it down once more over Roman Nose's shoulders. Rob hit the man on the side of the head with the club he had picked up, and the soldier slumped unconscious into the dirt of the road.

Rob slipped his knife from its case and sliced through the leather of the harness that bound Roman Nose to the wagon. Out of the corner of his eye, he could see a dozen or more wounded Britishers inside it. Some of them were trying to crawl free, but the rest lay tumbled one upon the other.

Then Roman Nose was on his feet, the cut ends of his harness dragging. Rob vaulted onto his back.

For a moment, there was no way to go. On every side the road was clogged with stumbling men. Then Rob saw a sudden opening—a clear shot at the roadside wall.

He kicked the bay in the ribs and stretched down low over his neck.

"Hay-yo! Roman Nose! Hup!"

The big gelding took the stone wall in one mighty leap and pounded up the side of the hill. There was a *bang!—bang!—bang!* of musket fire behind them. And then Roman Nose was breasting the top of the knoll from which Rob had started his mad run downhill.

Rob pulled the big bay up, and then slid off his back and put his arms around the thick neck.

"You old son of a gun!" he said. He slapped the horse's sweat-streaked sides and stroked his tangled mane. If he knew that tears were running down his cheeks, he didn't care. "You old, no-good son of a gun!"

[*173*]

Then he saw Sary. She was standing just where he had left her. There was a smile on her pale, freckled face.

"Sary," Rob said grandly, "get up on this horse behind me. We'll give you a ride home."

He climbed up on Roman Nose and pulled Sary up behind him. Roman Nose reached his big head around and tried to nibble Rob's toe.

Rob looked around once more at the shattered remnants of a once-proud British army that was stumbling down the Boston road in defeat.

Then he turned Roman Nose's head in the direction of Lexington Town.

CHAPTER THIRTEEN

George Washington's Army

ROB lounged on the broad front steps of Buckman's Tavern and listened to the war talk. That was all you heard when people got together these days. Here in Lexington, though, the war seemed a million miles away—almost as remote, he thought, as the big yellow moon that was coming up yonder over the tops of the elms and maples that edged the Green.

John Buckman had been right about the British. They hadn't tried to come back. The farmers who had taken down their muskets from over the fireplaces to fight at Concord Bridge and from behind the walls along the Bloody Road, had hung them up again and gone back to their spring plowing. Lexington was once again a peaceful country village, lazing in the warm New England sun.

But over in Cambridge, just twelve miles or so down the road, the war was as real as it had been in Lexington and Concord on that bright spring morning almost three months ago.

A new British army had been rushed out from England to reinforce General Gage in Boston. It was commanded by a man people called Gentleman Johnny Burgoyne. Just three weeks ago, Burgoyne and Gage had hurled their combined forces at a group of militiamen who had fortified Breed's Hill on the heights above Charlestown. And once more the British Regulars had broken against the Yankee guns and been beaten back in confusion—until the Americans had run out of powder and were forced to retreat across Charlestown Neck.

Now all the American colonies, from Maine to the Carolinas, were up in arms. General George Washington had come up from his plantation in Virginia to take command of the Colonial forces. And over on the Cambridge flats he was getting together an army—not a disorganized mob of Minute Men this time, but a Regular Army, fitted out with proper arms and proper uniforms.

Rob wondered how he'd look in a long blue uniform coat with white facings down the front. Well, he'd know first thing in the morning. His problem now was how to tell Uncle John—and Sary—what he had done this afternoon.

John Buckman was talking to two men who had stopped at the tavern for the night:

"Yes, sir! I served with George Washington out in Pennsylvany during the old French war. He was only a colonel then—not much older'n I was—but he knew more about fightin' than all the Redcoat gen'rals put together."

"They say he's got nigh ten thousand men over in Cambridge, and more comin' in every day," one of the travelers remarked.

"That's what they say," John Buckman agreed. "But ask the boy here. He drove a load of fresh vegetables over there today." He turned to Rob. "How many men do you reckon Colonel Washington's got, Rob?"

Rob grinned to himself in the darkness. Uncle John was making this easy.

"At least one more than he had this time yesterday."

"What do you mean by that, son?"

Rob gulped, and then he blurted it out:

"I joined up today."

"Oh, Rob!" Sary had been sitting in a big rocking chair in the shadows against the wall. She jumped up and clapped her hand to her mouth. "You *didn't!*"

"Yes, I did, Sary," Rob said. "I had to."

Without another word, Sary turned and ran into the house.

John Buckman eased himself up out of his chair.

"Come here, Rob," he said quietly.

Rob glanced around for Sary, but she was gone. He got up and walked across the porch.

"I know you asked me to wait till I was seventeen, Uncle John. But there was a sight of boys no older'n me wearing blue uniforms in Cambridge today. And I'll wager I've seen more fightin' than the lot of them."

"Yes, son," John Buckman said. "I'll risk a shilling that you have."

He held out his hand and grasped Rob's in a man's handshake.

"I knew you were bound to pack up and go sooner or later, Rob. And you've got my blessing."

[*178*]

"Roman Nose is saddled up out in the stable, Uncle John. I'd feel real kindly if you'd let me take him with me."

"He's your horse, son."

One of the strangers spoke up:

"You figurin' to join the Cav'ry, boy?"

"Well," Rob said, "most of the mounted troops in Cambridge, what few of them there are, came up from Virginia with General Washington. I aim to show 'em that Massachusetts men can ride horses as well as southerners."

"Then you're fixing to leave tonight, Rob?" John Buckman asked.

"That's so, Uncle John. I promised the recruiting sergeant I'd show up in Cambridge in the morning."

John Buckman reached into his waistcoat pocket and pulled out a fat gold watch.

"I'm proud of you, Rob. And your pa would be proud of you too. I wish he could have lived to see this day."

He held the watch out to Rob.

"Take this with you, son. It was your pa's. He told me to give it to you when you grew up to be a man."

Rob took the watch, and then there was a long moment of silence.

"Well," John Buckman said, "go along with you, boy. Say good-by to Mrs. Williams and Sary, and then get on your horse. You don't want to keep that sergeant in Cambridge waiting."

A flood of hot tears had welled up into Rob's eyes. Suddenly his throat felt so choked up that he was afraid to try to speak. He turned and went into the tavern.

In the kitchen, Mrs. Williams already had made him up a bundle of food.

"You may need it, Rob," she said. "They say the army's rations are short."

She stood on tiptoes and pecked him on the cheek.

"God bless you, son!" she said.

Rob looked around.

"Where's Sary?" he asked.

"She was here just a second ago," Mrs. Williams said. "Likely she'll be right back."

"I'll go out and get Roman Nose," Rob said. "Then I'll come back to tell her good-by."

Rob led the big bay horse out of the stable and up the path to the kitchen door.

Sary held a small object in her hand

A little figure stepped out from the shadow of a dogwood tree. The yellow moonlight gleamed on her yellow hair.

"Rob."

Sary held a small object in her hand.

"I've been keeping this to give you when you went away to war, Rob. Here, take it."

It was a leatherbound book.

"It's a Bible, Rob. Keep it with you. I wrote something in the front."

Shyly, she grasped his head in her two hands and kissed him quickly.

"Keep that with you, too," she said.

Then she disappeared into the shadows as abruptly as she had come out of them.

Rob stared after her for a moment. Then he opened the little Bible to the front page. But even the golden moonlight wasn't bright enough to read by.

He closed the book and put it into his pocket.

Well, he'd have to wait till morning light to read what Sary had written!

He climbed up on his horse and trotted down the road toward Cambridge and George Washington's army.

About the Author

FELIX SUTTON was born in Clarksburg, West Virginia, and is a graduate of West Virginia University. A former newspaper reporter, sports writer and editor, he has written more than a dozen books for young people—mostly on adventure, sports, and historical subjects. Among his most recent are WE WERE THERE AT PEARL HARBOR, DANGEROUS SAFARI, and HOT ROCK OF HONDO. He and Mrs. Sutton and their three children now live in Connecticut where he devotes as much time as he can to his favorite hobbies, hunting and fishing.

About the Artist

HERMAN B. VESTAL, a born New Yorker, now lives in Little Silver, New Jersey. He also has lived in North Carolina, Virginia, Florida, New Mexico, New York, and Montreal, Canada. He is a graduate of both the National Academy and the Pratt Institute. He was a U. S. Coast Guard Combat Artist in the European and Pacific Theaters from 1942 to 1945. Since then his work has appeared in such national magazines as *Everywoman's, Reader's Digest, American Rod and Gun,* and *Coronet.* In 1954, he was selected from the American Watercolor Society Show in New York as one of "America's Top 40 Artists."

About the Historical Consultant

EARL SCHENCK MIERS was graduated from Rutgers University and became editor of the University Publications of Rutgers. Later he became director of Rutgers University Press. He has made a lifelong study of American history and is considered an authority on both the Revolution and the Civil War. He is himself the author of many successful books both for adults and for young people, one of the most recent of the latter being WE WERE THERE WHEN WASHINGTON WON AT YORKTOWN.

WE WERE THERE BOOKS

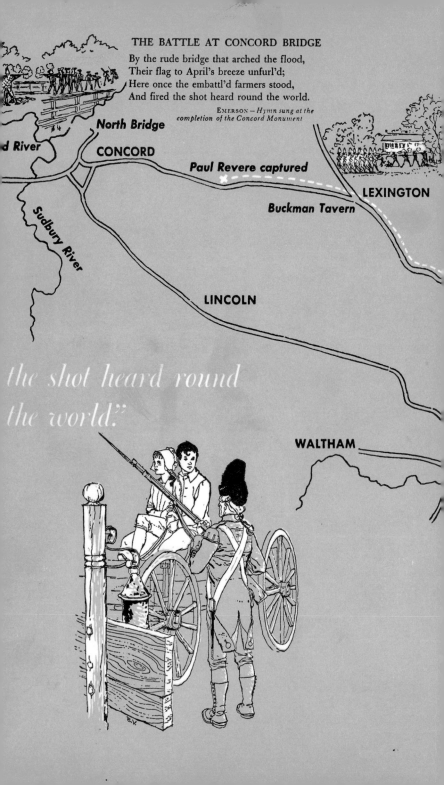

THE BATTLE AT CONCORD BRIDGE

By the rude bridge that arched the flood,
Their flag to April's breeze unfurl'd;
Here once the embattl'd farmers stood,
And fired the shot heard round the world.

EMERSON — *Hymn sung at the
completion of the Concord Monument*

North Bridge

CONCORD

d River

Paul Revere captured

Sudbury River

LEXINGTON

Buckman Tavern

LINCOLN

*the shot heard round
the world."*

WALTHAM

PAUL REVERE'S RIDE

"...One, if by land, and two, if by sea;
And I on the opposite shore will be,
Ready to ride and spread the alarm
Through every Middlesex village and farm,
For the country folk to be up and to arm."

LONGFELLOW

MEDFORD

Mystic River

MENOTOMY
(ARLINGTON)

WINNISIMMET

CHARLESTOWN

CAMBRIDGE

TERTOWN

arles River

BOSTON

OLD NORTH CHURCH

BROOKLINE

ATLANTIC OCE

DORCHESTER
NECK

ROXBURY

DORCHESTER